A cardboard box with a [illegible] two red Spider-Man legs [illegible] room. Harry insisted on carrying it with the flaps up so he could see inside. His eyes were streaming with tears. His mum guided him in with a hand across his back and helped him settle the box on the table. It was the first time Harry tipped his head up. He looked at me and his eyes filled with tears and emptied on his cheeks.

'Don't worry,' I said.

'I'm so sorry,' he said to me, as if I was a rabbit too.

'It's not your fault,' I said. 'This happens all the time.'

He wiped away his tears with the sleeve of his pyjama top. As I lifted Emily out of the box and studied her frazzled face I looked into Harry's eyes and I saw myself in his shoes, a little boy standing exactly where he was, in a veterinary surgery in Stanmore, north-west London . . .

Marc Abraham trained as a vet at Edinburgh University. After setting up his own veterinary practice, he became a veterinary advisor to the Kennel Club of Great Britain and is now the resident vet giving pet advice on ITV's *This Morning*, *Daybreak*, *My Pet Shame*, *BBC Breakfast*, Crufts and many other TV shows. Recently Marc was voted 'the UK's Favourite Vet' by the British public and has an iPhone app available for dog lovers called *Canine Care*. Marc campaigns a lot for animal welfare issues, especially against puppy farming. He lives in Brighton.

You can visit Marc at www.marcthevet.com

Pets in Need

Marc Abraham

RED FOX

PETS IN NEED
A RED FOX BOOK 978 1 849 41619 1

First published in Great Britain by Red Fox Books,
an imprint of Random House Children's Books,
A Random House Group Company

3 5 7 9 10 8 6 4 2

Adapted for younger readers from
Vet on Call: My First Year as an Out-of-Hours Vet, first published
in the UK in 2011 by Ebury Press, an imprint of Ebury Publishing
A Random House Group Company

The Random House Group Limited supports The Forest Stewardship Council (FSC®), the
leading international forest certification organisation. Our books carrying the FSC label are
printed on FSC® certified paper. FSC is the only forest certification scheme endorsed by the
leading environmental organisations, including Greenpeace. Our paper procurement
policy can be found at www.randomhouse.co.uk/environment

Red Fox Books are published by Random House Children's Books,
61–63 Uxbridge Road, London W5 5SA

www.**kids**at**randomhouse**.co.uk
www.**totallyrandombooks**.co.uk

Addresses for companies within The Random House Group Limited
can be found at: www.randomhouse.co.uk/offices.htm

THE RANDOM HOUSE GROUP Limited Reg. No. 954009

A CIP catalogue record for this book is available from the British Library.

Printed and bound by CPI Group (UK) Ltd, Croydon, CR0 4YY

*For my first cat, Suzy – in memory
of the adventures we had together*

Author's note

When most of you are tucked up in bed with hot water bottles and winter duvets pulled over your heads, I am hard at work. Imagine if your much-loved pet became sick in the middle of the night, at a time when the rest of the world is asleep – what do you do? Who do you call? The answer is *me* – the emergency vet. And when the animals arrive for urgent treatment, that's when my job really begins . . .

When I decided to set up my own night-time surgery, I had no idea what funny characters (human and animal!) I'd meet along the way. In the pages of this book you will find weird and wonderful stories. I've made sure to keep every detail as realistic as possible, so you can experience the rollercoaster ride that was my first year as an emergency vet. There's also a glossary at the back of the book to explain any medical terms that I've used, and a whole section on how to care for your own pets, too.

For anyone who loves animals, has a pet, or is even thinking of joining me in the crazy world of veterinary medicine one day – this book is for you.

MARC the VET
X

Chapter One
Rattling Chickens

Lack of sleep makes everything slow; it makes clocks and brains and bodies sluggish, and it makes it nigh on impossible to find anything good on television. In my years as an out-of-hours vet I found only one cure for sleepiness: the ringing telephone.

'Good evening, surgery.'

I rolled the last 'r' in 'surgery' unintentionally. After weeks of business plans and paperwork, meetings with the practice's partners, and meetings about more meetings, Ruth, the nurse, and I had finally established the emergency vet service that Brighton had so desperately needed. We had been up and running for ten or so days and we were still feeling our way along.

'Oh dear,' said a woman's husky voice on the end of the line.

Of all the possible greetings, that isn't one you want to hear.

'Oh dear, oh dear,' she repeated.

'It's OK,' I said, 'take a minute, you're speaking to the vet.'

She told me her name was Helen.

As Helen went into what was wrong, my eyes did a tour of the room. Any item of furniture that was flat enough was topped with greetings cards. *Good Luck with your new job*, read one, sitting high on the filing cabinet. *Don't muck it up*, read its neighbour. Our futuristic new LCD television blared unfuturistic eighties music videos. I gestured to Ruth, the practice's nurse, who was standing by, to turn the volume down. Helen was noticeably agitated. She huffed and puffed into the phone as she spoke. Her words came out chopped up.

'I'm in ever such a flap,' she said, 'I don't know what's happened to chickens.'

I paused and took a breath.

'To who?'

'To chickens,' she said.

'Chickens?' I asked, making triply sure I'd heard her right.

I waved at Ruth.

The television went off.

Over the next few minutes I asked Helen the best questions I could think of and listened hard to her answers. I pressed the receiver into my ear to help suck some clarity out of what she was saying. I flapped at Ruth for a scrap of paper, and fished in my pockets for a ballpoint pen. I had a crib sheet on the desk with some instructions. Take their name. I jotted down *Helen*. Who's the patient? *Chickens*, question mark, exclamation mark. It all went down. The next prompt was to ask what the problem was. Everything to date had been reasonably routine, and in most cases you can triage easily over the phone. Not this one.

'He *what* when he walks? Rattles?'

I stared at the A4 print-out that was Blu-Tacked to the wall – AN EMERGENCY TO YOU IS AN EMERGENCY TO US. I suppose you could call it our ethos. It was also the first thing I'd ever laminated. There was a wrinkle right through the middle.

'Why don't you pop down,' I said, 'and we'll take a look.'

I stood at the window and watched for Helen through the slats of the blind. It was February and the rain had set in, and not a little drizzle either. It was the sort of weather you see in commercials for hug-in-a-mug soups and hot chocolates; theatrical flashes of lightning, rumbles of thunder and a downpour that stuck fringes onto foreheads. I swilled a mouthful of bitter instant coffee. I had nightmarish visions of Helen pulling up in a van or a lorry, stacked from the floor to the ceiling with hundreds of cages, each occupied by a flapping bird. In my ten years as a professional vet so far I hadn't come across a single chicken, then ten days into my own surgery and – *bam!*

A pair of headlights bumped into the car park. The headlights didn't belong to a chicken lorry but to an old blue Volvo. The front door swung open and into a puddle stepped a tatty pair of sports shoes. The woman who climbed from the car had brown curly hair that was drenched by the rain. She quickly hopped out of the puddle and stepped in front of the headlights, turning her body into a silhouette. I opened the back door and called to her as the rain drummed on the flat roof.

'Do you want a hand bringing them in?' I shouted across the car park.

'*Them?*' she said.

There was a bark from the boot of her car.

'The birds?'

Helen fell quiet.

We swapped confused expressions for a moment.

'Birds?' she said. She made her way towards me. 'Birds?' she said again, with an almost laugh. 'Do you mean Chickens?'

'Chickens' was a golden retriever.

Ruth led the way through the back door into the consulting room. In the professional surroundings of the surgery, I saw Helen's shoulders visibly relax. I passed her a paper towel to wipe the rain out of her eyes. Chickens, a beautiful ten-month-old golden retriever puppy, didn't look happy. He waddled into the room and hunched by the table, bowing his head over his feathery chest, looking for all the world as if he was in prayer.

'He's been doing this since we came in from our walk,' said Helen, nervously scrunching the paper towel I gave her in her hand. 'And he comes down on his front legs like he's praying.'

She pressed her palms flat together as if uttering one of her own, then went back to scrunching the paper towel.

'Is he off his food?' I asked.

I looked up and saw Helen with her glasses off. Her wide eyes were frazzled. She looked like a little girl sitting on the teacher's chair at school. Without her coat she looked small and pensive and she sat with her hands open in her lap, palms now facing up to the ceiling. If I was to guess her occupation, I'd have gone for librarian. She nodded her head as she wiped her steamy spectacles with her polo shirt.

'He's been in his bed most of the day,' Helen said softly. 'I got him up, he did a couple of steps, then he does this' – she leaned forward and moved her

hands by her throat to suggest he was retching –
'but nothing comes out.'

Unproductive attempts to vomit, I noted to myself.

'Then I noticed when he started to walk that he made this rattling sound.' She looked down at Chickens standing there. 'He's not doing it now. I'll tell you what it sounded like.'

Helen got a set of keys out of her bag and bashed them against the counter. Then she silenced the jangling keys and rat-a-tat-tatted the plastic head against the countertop instead.

'No, that's not it.'

She furrowed her brow.

Helen reached for Chicken's collar and gave him a little tug. The retriever stumbled forwards.

'It's fine, Helen,' I said. 'Is he passing faeces?'

But she wouldn't let me finish. She walked him around the room. At first I heard nothing, but by the fifth or sixth step there was an audible sound. A faint *clunk clunk clunk* coming from his stomach.

'It's like salt pots bashing together,' she said.

I nodded as if I had some idea what that sounded like.

'Is he passing faeces?' I asked again.

'No, I don't think so.'

Chickens stopped and looked around, then stretched his neck and licked his sore stomach.

Ruth gave Helen a mug of black tea and helped her to a seat while I put on my gloves and knelt down beside her dog.

'Will you hold his bum?' I said.

Helen put the mug down on the floor and stretched forwards.

I ran my fingers under his belly and felt about his abdomen. As soon as I knelt down to examine him further, Chickens turned his head round and tried to grab the stem of my stethoscope, almost puncturing the thick rubber piping with his needle-sharp teeth.

'Not for you,' I said, tucking it into my scrubs.

'He'll eat anything,' Helen confirmed.

I got back to examining his abdomen. My fear was that he could have a gastric torsion, the 'golden emergency scenario' that would have been a real test after being open for just a few days. I threw a glance at Ruth; she looked worried. I ran my hand over Chickens's tender belly. At first everything felt fine, but then towards the back of his stomach, the part we call the caudal aspect, there was a bump, and then another, and one more. The stomach was protruding beyond the rear of the ribcage. Each lump was hard and spherical, each was a similar size, and when I pressed them the little dog whimpered. Helen was following everything I was doing, her eyes wide like saucers. I put my stethoscope in my ears and pressed the chestpiece onto his stomach. I find that a stethoscope can sometimes be more of a thinking device than anything else. It bought me some time to consider the options.

'It feels like there's something in his stomach,' I said.

'What?' she cried. 'What is it? Is it bad? Is it awful? Tell me it's not bad.'

'I think he's eaten something he shouldn't. What I'll do is perform an X-ray and then we'll be able to assess the situation.'

* * *

The X-ray took a while to perform. It was a conscious X-ray, which has the advantage of not having to use sedation, so it's usually both quicker and safer. But with a lively puppy like Chickens it can be a fairly testing procedure as it relies on the patient lying still on the plate, not something that came easily to Chickens.

'He's a livewire, isn't he, Helen?' I said, as Ruth clipped the X-ray onto the light box.

Helen nodded. She was understandably tense.

I walked over to the light box and flicked the switch. The neon tube behind it flickered on. Foreign-body ingestion can usually be easily confirmed with an X-ray, depending on what the swallowed object actually is. Hard, dense objects like bone or metal show up much better than softer objects like rubber or plastic. This one was very clear. Imagine shining a torch back at you through a big balloon, a balloon that contained a bunch of black grapes. There was a cluster of black circles, each one larger than a fifty-pence piece. They were clustered at the base of the stomach.

'Oh, no!' Helen said. 'Oh dear!'

'Helen, can I ask you a question?'

She nodded.

'Do you live near a golf course?'

Pre-med, propofol injectable anaesthetic, intravenous drip and in we go. We positioned Chickens on his back, fast asleep, with his legs tied down. It was straight through the mid-line to his stomach to perform a gastrostomy, literally a hole in his stomach to remove the offending items. Two and half hours on the operating table and sixty-seven stitches. I thought he might have swallowed three or four of them but when we opened him up there were *nine* golf balls, all turned brown by the acid in his stomach. It was unbelievable. Each golf ball was four centimetres in diameter and weighed close to 50 grams. I had never seen anything remotely close to that size in a dog's stomach. With nearly half a kilogram of them rattling around in his stomach it was no wonder Chickens was praying. I repaired the gastric wall with a couple of layers of inverting sutures, flushed the abdominal cavity with a few drip-bags worth of warm saline, and Chickens came round from his anaesthetic very smoothly. After a night in the hospital, with Ruth and me desperately trying to stop him chewing his drip out of his leg using combinations of buster collars and more bandages, and then keeping down small portions of chicken and rice over the next twenty-four hours, he was collected by his whole family and went home.

When I arrived at the surgery the following day there was a bunch of flowers waiting for me. The receptionist had cut their stems and left them standing in the kitchen sink. On the front, written in black fountain pen, was a little yellow card. *Good luck with the new surgery.* I flipped it over. There wasn't a name, but there was something else written on the back: *Don't count your Chickens before they've hatched.* I smiled to myself as I pinned the card to the corkboard in the common room. I had a feeling I'd see him again soon.

Chapter Two
Early Birds

Brighton is a large town with a two-legged population of about 150,000. When I decided to open my clinic, there were several veterinary practices but there was little provision for out-of-hours vets. I'd worked in clinics with them before, one in Cardiff and another a few miles down the road, and had seen first-hand how it could transform a business. Brighton was crying out for another emergency service that ran on nights and weekends. So, after a meeting with one of Brighton's busy veterinary practices, the partners agreed to re-jig a few filing cabinets at their premises to make room for myself and a nurse.

On our first day, Ruth and I agreed it would be a good idea to arrive early. Strange as it may seem, I had only been inside the surgery once before. It was a plain brick building with automatic doors and a fish tank in the waiting room; that was as much as I could remember. We weren't expecting balloons and WELCOME, MARC AND RUTH! banners, but I think we both thought there'd be some sort of special greeting when we walked up to the hatch. Nobody so much as looked up.

'Is it Gloria?' I asked the bouffant hair behind reception.

'Depends who's asking,' said its owner, her head very much in her work, filing something away in a folder.

'It's Marc,' I said, 'and Ruth.' I paused. 'We're due to meet George?'

Gloria froze. Her head came up and she looked us up and down, as if inspecting prospective suitors for her daughter. Suddenly everything changed.

'Gloria,' she said over the top of her reading glasses, and she held out her hand.

We made our introductions. Neither of us realized this at the time, but the sight of her face in the mornings would be like a glimpse of an

approaching passenger ship to a desert island cast-
away. Gloria was a relief in every possible sense.
We'd take the practice off her hands at six every
night and hand it back to her at eight the next morning. Working weekends meant six o'clock Friday to
eight o'clock Monday with no break in between. So
on a Monday morning at eight o'clock, there was
no word in the English language more welcome
than *Gloria*.

Gloria led us through to the back room, where
George and Edward were waiting.

'Marc! Ruth!' George cried, leaping to his feet.
'Welcome, welcome, welcome.'

George was the senior partner at the practice
and had a habit of repeating words for effect. He
and Edward were like chalk and cheese. Edward was
quite possibly the most serious man I've ever met.
He owned three calculators but no mobile phone.

'Well,' said George, 'let's give you the grand tour.'

We went on a ten-minute wander through a
series of interconnected rooms. George insisted on
leading the way like a hyperactive tour guide. No
object escaped a remark.

'The kettle,' he said with a flourish. 'I imagine that will see some action.'

He looked at us expectantly; we gave him a small smile.

The tour party moved on to a door marked NECESSARIUM, which housed a toilet and a basin.

'And now, the room we saved till last,' said George. He locked eyes with the pair of us. 'Your new home.'

As he uttered those words he flung open the door and semi-bowed. When he straightened up he made a sweep of his hand and showed off the room like a magician's assistant. Edward appeared behind him, looking characteristically dour. The space they had made available was for our own exclusive use. It was a room about three by three metres that had had many past lives, most recently a storage room, as the dusty pink carpet, a bright pink trim around the edge where archiving boxes had once sat, testified. There were no windows; the only light came from a pair of fluorescent tubes. The partners had moved in one desk, one swivel chair, one very low easy chair and a military green filing cabinet. There was a calendar tacked to the wall. And that was it. Not exactly cosy, but it was fine for our needs.

'Thank you, guys,' I said, setting down my rucksack.

Four pairs of eyes peered around the room looking for something that ought to be said, or that needed to be done. Edward broke the silence.

'Well, I suppose we should leave you both to settle in. If you need anything, just ask,' he said mechanically.

The partners smiled and shuffled out, pulling the door shut behind them. Ruth and I swapped glances, then our eyes drifted over to the clock on the wall, which had pictures of cats painted around the rim. There was a different breed occupying the position that a number would normally be. The second hand worked its way round to the top. We traced its last steps from a grey British shorthair, 56, 57, 58, 59, to a Siamese. I raised my eyebrows. Ruth managed a heart-felt 'Hurray'. It was like New Year's Eve all over again. There was no singing or fireworks, but like New

Year's it was a teeny bit of an anticlimax. Nothing had changed and nothing was different. There weren't owners hammering at the doors. The phone switchboard didn't start flashing red. The phone didn't ring at all.

'Here's to us,' I said, raising an empty desk-tidy.

Ruth laughed, and raised an imaginary glass to me.

My eyes skirted around the room to find something else to comment on, but returned without finding anything funny.

Ruth scrunched up her nose. 'How long d'you think before it rings?' she said.

I shrugged. 'But if it doesn't, we could take turns to call in and pretend.'

'What's that noise?' I woke up with a start; my bleary eyes peered around the room. I was slumped over the desk in a swivel chair, no idea what the time was. And then it went again. I stared at the grey plastic thing in front of me.

'Ruth!' I shouted. 'It's ringing!'

There was a squeal of delight from the kitchen, followed by the sound of Ruth's hurried steps down the corridor. *Take a breath, Marc. Keep calm*, I told myself and placed my hand on the receiver.

'Good evening, surgery,' I said.

Ruth huddled round, wide-eyed with expectation.

Then a voice said, 'What's on specials?'

'Excuse me?'

'We want one chicken korma, a balti, two pilau, two peshwari naans and an aloo gobi.'

Our first proper patient arrived at a quarter past three.

'He's here!' Ruth yelled down the hall. 'I'll put the kettle on.'

To say it came as a relief would be an understatement. In nine hours the telephone had only rung three times, and two of those were for Indian takeaways. So whether this patient could have waited until the morning was neither here nor there; we weren't about to turn them away.

As soon as I saw the clients arrive I opened the

door to the car park and began to walk out towards them, determined to show our first patients a warm reception. Anxious to convey the magnitude of their visit, I gripped the owner firmly by the hand and let him know they were our first.

'We're night-shift virgins,' I said.

It may not have come across as reassuring, but this owner didn't seem to mind. Bill was a Hell's Angel. He had pulled up on a Harley Davidson motorbike, an immaculately polished silver and blue tourer. He took off his open-faced helmet and shook out his long silver hair as if we were shooting a shampoo commercial. On the back of his leather jacket was the famous winged-skull logo and the slogan: HELLS ANGELS FOREVER. Bill had an unlikely passenger. On the back of the bike at the end of the leather seat, secured with two yellow bungee cords, was a birdcage cloaked in a thick blanket.

'What's his name?' I asked, lifting the cloth for a peek.

Bill looked me straight in the eye.

'Pretty Boy,' he said, without a trace of irony.

I nodded and swallowed a smile. Best to keep the 'Pets look like their owners' joke to myself.

Pretty Boy was a beautiful green and yellow budgerigar. His head was tucked under his wing and his feathers were fluffed out. Although budgerigars are usually healthy, robust creatures, they are susceptible to several minor ailments and a few of a somewhat more serious nature. The floor of his cage was caked in diarrhoea. This can be a tell-tale sign of enteritia, a condition caused by a run-down liver.

Ruth greeted Bill with a steaming mug of tea and the four of us headed off down the corridor to the consulting room.

There were two consulting rooms in the surgery. They were roughly the size of a medium-sized bedroom in a terraced house. We went into Consulting Room Two. There were posters on the walls – PARASITE PROTECTION MADE EASY, one of a laminated diagram of a rabbit's digestive tract, and another of feline dentition. There were weighing scales, a fridge and a photo board with snaps of patients sent in by their owners.

I took my place behind the table and put on a pair of gloves. The strip light flickered above me. Any vet will tell you that budgies are notoriously hard to hold, examine and medicate. They can become stressed very easily and it's not uncommon for them to suffer a fatal cardiac arrest when held by their vet or even their owner. So Ruth set about making the room as stress-free as possible. Without saying a word she dimmed the lights to a lower level, shut the door and made sure all the escape routes were closed. I was wearing rubber gloves so as to reduce the chances of infection. We were set. With a flip of a catch I opened the cage and took the bird in my fingers. Bill craned in to look. The budgie didn't object; enteritia usually makes a bird tame. Contrary to popular mythology – see 'bird-brained' in the dictionary – budgerigars are an intelligent species. So perhaps Pretty Boy knew where he was, and sensed that the fingers that were smoothing his feathers and untucking his head meant him no harm.

'Do you feed him anything other than seeds?'

Bill shook his head. 'Not really.'

Pretty Boy's fluffed-up appearance suggested that he'd been ill for over twenty-four hours. Luckily he was still drinking so his prognosis wasn't as guarded as other poorly budgies I'd examined before. I moved a cotton bud in front of him, which usually never fails to bring on a biting frenzy, but Pretty Boy didn't flicker. It was clear that he was deteriorating fast and needed sorting out immediately. Ignoring a disease like enteritia can frequently be fatal.

'You don't feed him anything sugary or starchy? A lot of owners give them crisps,' I said. 'You know, as a treat every now and then.'

A little colour swept into Bill's face. He glanced at the floor.

'For other owners it's biscuits. Break the corner off a bourbon, poke it through the bars.'

Bill swung his motorcycle boot over the tiles, as if trying to shoe an invisible cat. Then he slowly lifted his face up.

'I, er, do give him the odd bite of cake,' he admitted. 'Now and then.'

'Now and then?'

I had visions of the macho biker in a chintzy floral front room, pouring a cup of Darjeeling from a tea set complete with a cosy, and delicately cutting a budgie-sized pyramid of Battenberg with a cake fork.

'Well, perhaps more than I should.'

And there was the answer.

The cause of enteritia is an internal one, commonly brought on by simply not feeding your budgie correctly with the right food like normal seed but instead letting them eat 'junk food' titbits such as cake, potato and other such foods that are particularly sugary and starchy. This in turn causes the liver to be overtaxed, run down and results in awful diarrhoea.

It is difficult to find a good bird vet. The focus in vet schools has always primarily focused on cats and dogs and large animal medicine. Unfortunately you hear stories of veterinarians 'winging it'. The majority of cases I see are routine and common conditions, but I will always call an avian specialist if something comes up that stumps me.

Ruth and I waved goodbye to Bill and Pretty Boy from the back step. Enteritia is simple enough to treat. I told Bill to cover three sides of the cage and sit the bird by the fire, letting him rest. And with a little bismuth carbonate sprinkled over his seed he'd be chirping away in no time. Bill secured the birdcage back in place with the bungee cords, and with a low growl and a roar the happy couple in the leather jacket and blanket disappeared off into the night.

Chapter Three
The Cat Who Laid an Egg

On our second day we'd barely hung up our coats when the practice phone rang. It was chucking it down outside and the thick donkey jacket I'd been wearing didn't offer much in the way of protection. I had taken off my trainers and was putting on my rubber clogs when Ruth knocked on the door and entered without waiting for an answer.

'Marc, will you speak to this lady?'

Ruth's expression screamed 'urgent', so I fastened up my scrubs as we tripped down the corridor. Ruth leaned against the doorframe as I took a seat in the office. The phone receiver was lying on the desk. I took a little breath and turned in my chair so that I could read Ruth's face and so she could see mine. The caller was Portuguese. Not only did she have a thick accent but also a limited English vocabulary. She ended each sentence with my name – 'Mr Abraham' – and her intonation rose as if she was pleading with me.

'She's howling?' I said.

'Can you hear it, Mr Abraham?'

The lady held the phone up and I heard nothing for a while, then came a low, whiny yowl.

'Did you hear it, Mr Abraham?' she said again. 'She pacing, pacing, pacing. Up and down. Up and down.'

'Is she pregnant?' I asked.

There was a pause on the end of the line.

'She is tortoise.'

'Tortoise?' I asked.

'Tortoise cat,' she said.

'No, I meant, is she pregnant, er, is she going to have kitten babies?' I asked.

'Maybe,' she said. 'How can they tell, Mr Abraham?'

It's not uncommon for owners not to notice that their pet is pregnant until very late on.

'She is fat,' she said. 'She is very fat. I kneel down, Mr Abraham.'

I listened as the owner knelt on the floor

beside her cat. There was a clunk as she knocked the receiver against the floor. She held the phone close to the cat so I could hear a rhythmical purring.

'That's good,' I said.

'Oooh,' said the lady, 'she's making milk.'

There are many signs that a cat is about to give birth. Typical things you might notice can include anxious, restless behaviour as the mother searches for a place to give birth. Vigilant owners will monitor the cat's temperature too, as approaching birth it will usually fall by a degree or so from normal. I think the penny must have dropped because I heard the lady squeal.

'Oh my *God*! Mr Abraham,' she said. 'Oh my GOD!' The kitten bombshell had just exploded across the phone line.

'It's fine,' I said. 'Why don't you sit down?'

I coached her over to her kitchen chair.

'Are you OK?' I asked.

She was jittering with a cocktail of emotions, two parts fear to one part excitement. She had been difficult to understand at the beginning of the conversation but now I was having trouble letting her know what she should do. I spoke very slowly.

'Have you had cats before?' I asked.

'No, Mr Abraham, is neighbour's,' she said.

'Is your neighbour there?' I tried.

Ruth's eyes went wide as she tried to make sense of things from only hearing one side of the conversation.

'No, Mr Abraham, is away,' said the lady.

'He's away? For how long?'

I expected her to tell me they'd popped out for a pint of milk or were away for a day or two.

'For six months,' came her reply. 'How do I make babies come?'

I could understand her panic. This was not her area of expertise. I learned later that the lady's neighbour was a marketing consultant and had been sent by his company to work in their big office in Philadelphia. He was understandably wary about taking his cat to a foreign country, especially when he had to be working so much and travelling round the East Coast, so he had asked her if she would mind cat-sitting. It turned out that she had only been doing this for a month, and never having looked after a cat before was coming across a whole new set of experiences. I tried to reassure her that problems during pregnancy and birth for cats are extremely rare in all breeds, apart from Persians perhaps, and in my experience over ninety-nine per cent of moggies deliver their kittens without assistance or complications.

'Best thing is not to disturb her,' I said. 'Give her some space. But maybe leave the door open so you can monitor things.'

The cat was undoubtedly fine; it was the poor cat-sitter I was worried about.

'How long should I wait?' she asked.

Ruth went outside to greet a dog owner who had arrived in the car park while I explained the full ins and outs of the birthing process to the Portuguese cat-sitter, letting her know what to expect so there weren't any further surprises. I talked her through everything, how the first kitten should arrive within an hour after the onset of labour, and how sometimes labour lasts only a few minutes before the kitten arrives.

'Other kittens should arrive with an interval of ten minutes to an hour between them,' I said. 'Everything should be fine, but call me if you have any trouble.'

Our second night could not have been more different to the first. Patients were in and out of the surgery as if a neon sign had been planted in the car park. Our phone did not stop from six p.m. till midnight.

We saw another budgie, this time with a feather cyst.

We saw a beautiful black Labrador called Sparky who, catching a whiff of a rabbit, had dived under a Land Rover and opened a seven-centimetre wound along his back. I shaved a twelve-by-five-centimetre rectangle of fur from around the wound, much to the proud owner's chagrin, and tidied-up fresh edges to make a clean stitch. The owner, in Barbour jacket and wellington boots, complimented my 'nice piece of embroidery' and suggested that next time I should shave something cool into Sparky's fur, like *Paws Rock!*

We saw a dog called Odie, who'd been rubbing his bottom along the carpet. He had an anal gland that needed emptying.

We had a cat that had eaten his sister's biscuits and suffered an allergic reaction. Harry was one of those cats that ate anything he could find, and it was a full-time job for his owners to make sure that he only ate the food that was for him. He had skin lesions right the way down his back that he scratched with his hind paws until they were red raw. I clipped around the area and applied an ointment before wrapping his feet in bandages to stop it getting any worse. It came as a shock for Harry, who then slipped around the treatment table like a foal on an ice rink.

'She's on the phone again,' said Ruth.

'Who?' I asked.

'The Portuguese woman.'

Ruth passed me the phone. I hadn't even got it up to my ear before the woman asked, 'Mr Abraham. Can I poke finger in her?'

I was taken aback.

'*No,*' I said. 'Absolutely not. Leave her where she is. Are there any kittens yet?'

'No,' said the lady. 'She move to the bedroom, Mr Abraham. I follow her from a distance and spy on her.'

'Where are you now?' I asked.

'Outside the bedroom – you tell me not to disturb. Shall I go in?' she said.

'I imagine she was just looking for a nice warm place to have them,' I said. 'Don't take it personally but she'd probably rather you weren't around. It's OK to have a peek and check on things, though.'

'Can I now?' she asked.

'Go on,' I said. 'I'll stay on the line.'

It went quiet for a minute. Then there was a gasp, the sound of the phone dropping to the carpet and an ear-piercing screech. It was a long-held note that lasted for a few seconds. The lady was no longer holding the phone but I could still hear her.

'There's an egg, Mr Abraham, I see an EGG!' she said.

When she picked up the receiver again I tried to calm her down.

'Sssshh,' I said, 'you'll frighten her.'

'It's an *egg*,' she said hysterically. 'An egg. Oh. MY. GOD. There isn't a baby inside.'

'It's a placenta,' I said firmly.

'No,' she said, 'an egg.'

I was wondering whether I'd have to explain to her that cats do not lay eggs; as far as I know there are only three mammals that do – the platypus, the short-beaked echidna and the long-beaked echidna (also known as spiny anteaters). But she didn't want a biology lesson.

'Oh. MY. *GOD*,' she said.

'It's a placenta.'

'An *egg*,' she repeated. 'There isn't a baby inside.'

We toed and froed for a couple of minutes, but she simply wouldn't have it.

'An *EGG!*, Mr Abraham,' she insisted.

'Don't panic,' I said finally. 'Have you got a car?'

Ruth and I couldn't leave the surgery in busy periods, and struggling to know what else to say I invited her in to see me with both the mother and her 'egg'.

Close to five in the morning the Portuguese woman arrived in a taxi. It was one of those ordinary saloon cars. They're white and green in Brighton. Before it had even come to a stop, the door was flung open and she came charging towards us. In one arm she carried a cat carrier, in the other a plastic bag. She was short, with thick dark hair and hazel eyes. Instead of using the bell, she rapped on the front door with her knuckles until Ruth came running to her assistance. She introduced herself as Mrs Lopez before pushing the carrier towards me.

'Is mother in the basket, Mr Abraham,' she said. 'Is egg in the bag, Mr Abraham.'

I peeked into the cat carrier; the mother hissed. She was a beautiful tortoiseshell queen. She was lying on her stomach, not on her side, and she wasn't in labour any longer, I was sure about that. She looked exhausted. I looked at the new mother then back to her cat-sitter. Mrs Lopez thrust a carrier bag under my nose, but kept hold of the handles.

'It was in the wardrobe,' she said.

She opened the bag so I could see inside.

'I open bedroom door and find this in wardrobe, Mr Abraham.'

I stared down into the white plastic carrier bag and saw the greenish placenta at the very bottom.

'Mrs Lopez, did you see any kittens in the wardrobe?'

She looked at me and shook her head. 'It is full of clothes and boots, Mr Abraham.'

I put my hand on her shoulder. 'I think we better take a proper look.'

It was our first home visit. The lady lived in a block of flats not far from the practice. It was one of those unattractive buildings from the seventies, named something like *Sandringham* or *Weston*. She lived on the top floor and the lift wasn't working so we hurried up the stairs – I counted seventy-nine – Mrs Lopez leading the way with her cat carrier, me behind, and Ruth bringing up the rear with the carrier bag.

'This is the bedroom,' she said, flinging open the

door. It was a small chintzy room containing a big pine double bed with a white duvet and floral throw, a pink side table with hundreds of photos in different-sized frames, a pine dresser against the wall and a huge pine wardrobe.

'Sssh!' said Ruth. 'Do you hear that?'

Mrs Lopez set down the cat carrier and knelt on the floor.

'*Eeeeee!*' went the wardrobe.

Mrs Lopez's eyes came out on stalks.

'*Eeeeee!*' it went again.

I didn't move. Neither did Ruth. Mrs Lopez crawled on hands and knees across the garish pink rug towards the wardrobe. She stopped and looked around.

'Open it,' I whispered.

Mrs Lopez reached forward and touched the corner of the door with her fingers. She picked at the underside and gently pulled it towards her.

'*Eeeeee!*' It was more than one voice.

We all crept closer to have a look inside. Very carefully Mrs Lopez swept aside some of the dresses that were hanging on the rack. The kitten cries grew louder. And standing just behind her, we watched Mrs Lopez crumble, as right at the back of the wardrobe was the most precious of things: a litter of five baby kittens.

That sight could warm the hardest of hearts. Ruth and I spent half an hour with Mrs Lopez and the kittens. We told her what she had to watch out for, and showed her how to care for them. It was best to leave them where they were for now and reunite them with their mum. Mrs Lopez said she was going to call one of the fattest ones Marc and the thin one Ruth. I wasn't sure whether to be flattered or offended.

Chapter Four
The Gerbil Lady

Let me tell you about the day I became Brighton's first and foremost gerbilologist, if such a thing exists.

The practice had been up and running for a couple of months when I took the call. As a vet you meet a lot of characters, and Fleur was something of a local celebrity. An ardent Brighton and Hove Albion fan, she would regularly turn up to the practice on a windswept Tuesday night in a replica shirt and scarf with a patient to drop off before the football match. She was my most regular client. This had something to do with the fact that she kept well over a hundred gerbils. Which, obviously, was how she came to be known to us as the 'Gerbil Woman'.

On the day I was to establish my gerbil credentials, Ruth and I pulled up outside Fleur's house in my sweet red Cinquecento. The practice phone had been diverted to Ruth's mobile and we had Blu-Tacked a laminated notice to the front door – BACK IN A LITTLE WHILE. Ruth had insisted on drawing a picture of a 'See you later' alligator underneath it. Fleur lived in the very last house of a quiet residential road. From the front it looked like any normal suburban house, but if you were able to see a satellite image of the property the first thing you'd notice would be the large black extension stretching out of the back of the house, and two large sheds, which served as aviaries.

Fleur's husband, Roger, ran an animal rescue centre. 'Ran' is maybe too soft a word for it. This was not a nine-to-five job: Roger devoted his entire life to the care and rescue of animals. From rehabilitating seagull chicks that had blown off townhouse roofs, and pigeons attacked by the peregrine falcons of Sussex Heights, a famous block of flats in town overlooking the West Pier, to unlucky fledglings snatched by worried owners from their cat's jaws. Roger and Fleur's house was not so much a home as a sanctuary for wild animals. Their garage was like one of those huge stuffed-bird displays at the Natural History Museum but with a hundred heartbeats and various whistles, chirps and pips, which got louder with every approaching tweezer of cat food. People would drop by with seagulls and swifts, but also hedgehogs and badgers and fox cubs and strays, and would think nothing of ringing their doorbell at ten o' clock, midnight, even two in the morning. It was inconvenient at times but Fleur and Roger wouldn't have it any other way.

We parked behind their little blue Metro in the drive. They had a large seagull sticker on the rear window: the emblem of the football club they loved and a bird that was more than a recurring theme in their lives. Ruth and I stood outside the front door rubbing our hands together to keep them warm.

'Hello, Marc,' said Fleur, and she leaned in for a hug.

Our breath made vapour trails in the air.

Fleur was a wonderful woman. Short, huggy and warm like a radiator. She was bursting with a passion and love for life, though nothing could quite top her love for gerbilkind. Fleur was more than a breeder, she was a gerbil evangelist, with a website dedicated to their upkeep, and her own gerbil version of the Ten Commandments, which she laminated and gave to every new owner. When she opened the door we were greeted by a newborn curled in the palm of her hand. It made embracing a little tricky. I went for a sort of side-hug.

'Come in, come in,' she said. 'The kettle's boiled, I'll just be a second. Tea?'

'Thank you,' I said.

Ruth was a few steps behind me. When she saw the baby gerbil peeking out of Fleur's hand she melted into a mushy puddle and let out a cutesy 'awwwwwww' before asking for a 'stwoke'.

We warmed our hands and toes by the gas fire as Fleur steeped the tea. Ruth looked wistfully towards the kitchen and made coochy-coo faces. Their house was an Aladdin's cave of animal affection. There were paintings and photographs in every conceivable place, clocks, ornaments and cuddly toys. There were gerbil plates, gerbil mugs and gerbil draught excluders.

Fleur chinked and clinked away in the kitchen,

but over and above it you could hear the sound of animal industry – the pitter-patter of five hundred tiny feet. Ruth's eyes flicked from one corner of the room to the other as she tried to work out where it was coming from. I nodded towards the pair of inter-connecting doors. The dining room was something else. Ruth had never been in the house before, but I'd warned her about the dining room on the drive over.

'The sound alone,' I'd told her, 'is like nothing you've ever heard.'

For all the animal goings-on, the household had a restful air. It's something that you often find with people who are doing what they were put on this earth to do. Fleur and Roger had one of those star-crossed stories. They had met on a late-night show for BBC Southern Counties Radio where Roger had been a guest presenter. They still produce a radio show every month called *Roger's World* and record it in their home studio. Roger presents while Fleur operates the controls and chips in every now and then. They make a wonderful team, and they've been doing it long enough for each to know what the other wants without so much as word passing between them.

Fleur pushed herself up on the balls of her toes and looked out of the living-room window as she came back with mugs of steaming tea.

'I'm sorry you had to make the trip out in this,' she said, looking out into the frost. 'Roger had a call from a lady about a badger and had to use the van, so I couldn't come over myself.'

Ruth was hoping a little face might be peeking out of a fold or a pocket in her sweater, but Fleur must have put the baby gerbil somewhere else. She set our mugs down on the coffee table on World Wildlife Fund coasters.

'That was when I noticed something was wrong,' she said. 'I'm sorry, what am I doing? Let's take them through.'

Fleur picked the mugs back up off the coasters and pushed them into our hands.

'You're OK carrying them, aren't you? We're in here. Marc, you've been here before, haven't you?'

I took a little slurp.

The dining room was separated from the living

room by two white sliding doors with frosted glass panels. With a little tug, Fleur pulled them open and I watched Ruth's face light up like a Christmas tree.

They still called it the dining room though it had long stopped playing that role. Three of the four walls served as apartment blocks for gerbils. They were like four-star, high-rise gerbil hotels. Gerbils are social creatures so Fleur had divided them into breeding pairs and allocated them their own love nests, complete with water bottles, twin beds and exercise equipment. There were 154 of them in total. Each cage was labelled, with their names – which usually began with an 'S' – painted onto a nameplate, which was cut into the shape of a rainbow and hung underneath the cage. The cages themselves were decorated with clip-art that had been cut and pasted from the internet. These gerbils lived in luxury. I'm sure Fleur would have wired in little telephones and mini-bars if the gerbils could use them. Every day each pair was allocated a few minutes to stretch their legs and run on a purpose-built gerbil gym while their love nests were given a thorough clean out and inspected for new arrivals.

The sight of the accommodation itself was a spectacle to behold, but it was the sound that really hit you. Gerbils are not noisy animals, but with 154 all talking, playing, drinking, squeaking and running round their wheels at once, the sound was other-worldly, like we were trespassing amongst the Lilliputians. Ruth hurried straight over to the cages and was going along them like a child in a pet shop.

'You'll have to excuse her,' I said. 'I wasn't aware that she had such a thing for gerbils.'

'No,' said Fleur, 'it's quite understandable.'

'I wuv their wittle fwaces,' said Ruth, pushing her own up to the cage.

Fleur was beaming. 'Do you keep gerbils?' she said.

'When I was growing up,' Ruth told her, moving on to the next cage.

I felt bad about separating the furry rock stars from their latest adoring fan, but there was a pressing matter to attend to. One of Fleur's gerbils was in a protracted labour. Shirley had been having contractions for over twenty-four hours without delivering. A gerbil usually rests for fifteen minutes between deliveries to conserve energy, but a wait of this duration was a sure sign something was seriously wrong.

'I'm assuming there isn't a chance of saving the babies,' said Fleur.

Shirley was lying on the straw at the bottom of a tank. Her teeth were chattering in pain. I looked up at Fleur, concern written all over her face.

'And she's been like this for a day?' I said.

'Almost two,' Fleur replied quietly.

'OK,' I said, pausing. 'Fleur, I have to warn you, but after two days I don't think – I mean, I might be wrong – but I think it's unlikely this will be good news for the babies.'

'I thought so,' said Fleur. 'That's fine. I just want Shirley to be all right.'

'The thing is, Fleur,' I said, 'she might not be all right if the babies are stuck inside.'

I looked into Fleur's eyes. They were strong and stubborn.

'That's why you're here,' she said. She paused, stretched out her hand and gently squeezed my arm. 'I've done my research and I know it's really uncommon. Most vets wouldn't touch this, and I understand why, but I'd love it if you could perform a Caesarean.'

I gulped. 'A Caesarean?'

I wanted to make sure I had heard her correctly. In the veterinary world you almost never hear the words 'gerbil' and 'Caesarean' in the same sentence, let alone be asked to perform one.

I looked from Shirley to Fleur and from Fleur to Shirley, and a lump the size of a gobstopper grew in the back of my throat. Though I had never done anything like it or, for that matter, heard of such a surgery being performed, there was no way I could stand in this woman's home and refuse her, and before I even knew what was happening I heard these words leaving my mouth:

'Ruth, could you fetch my bag from the car?'

Fleur's big eyes welled up with tears.

As much as I would have liked it, my bag was not

one of those old leather doctor's bags that the medics in *Poirot* carry. It was a large plastic box with tiers of shelves inside, such as a fisherman or an electrician might have. There are a great many tools to carry on a home visit. Usually we would have some idea what case we were about to see and pack accordingly, but Fleur had been reluctant to explain the nature of the problem over the phone, for reasons that were now painfully obvious.

Ruth took Fleur to the living room to sign the consent forms, while I racked my brains to try to remember what they had taught me at vet school. I don't know if there was ever a lecture on small animal Caesareans, but if there had been I must have been off that day. I looked at the gerbil sitting next to my hand. Shirley was no more than fifteen centimetres long, including her tail, which made up almost half her length. The incision I was going to make would be absolutely minute. If you've ever made an Airfix model plane, you'll appreciate what I mean when I say it was fiddly. I searched around in my bag for the smallest, thinnest scalpel blade I could find and placed it on the top of the table. The other trouble was anaesthetizing her. Small animals are usually put under by placing them inside a container and introducing gas into it. Normally I'd use a plastic box in the practice to make a small chamber, but because we didn't know what we were coming to we hadn't brought one with us.

'Fleur,' I asked. 'Do you by any chance have a clean margarine tub?'

'Hmm,' she said, 'I don't know.'

'I need a tub of sorts, to put Shirley to sleep.'

'Hang on,' she said. 'I'll be right back.'

Fleur nipped off to the kitchen. I looked at Ruth through the gap in the connecting doors, kneeling by the coffee table, and I looked at the scalpel blade, and I looked around at the gerbil tower blocks and began to regret saying, 'I'll do it,' with quite the bravado I had. I mean, where do you start? It was my Superman complex kicking in. Riding in like a knight in shining scrubs on my big white stallion. Maybe I was being too hard on myself. This was about Fleur and Shirley, and I knew that if I didn't operate, Shirley would die, so there really was no other option.

'Ice cream, anyone?' said Fleur, swinging into the living room with a newly washed-out tub. 'Raspberry Ripple,' she said. 'I've scooped it into a bowl if you fancy some after.'

This wasn't the time to start contemplating dessert. I looked down at Shirley on the table and back up to Fleur again.

'Look,' I said, 'I want you to know that I'll give it my best shot, but I've never done this before . . .'

'Don't worry,' Fleur insisted. 'I wouldn't have called you if I didn't think she'd be in the best possible hands.'

We put the pregnant gerbil under in the ice-cream tub that served as an anaesthetizing chamber, and as Fleur stroked Shirley's soft fur with the tip of her finger I clipped carefully around the gerbil's abdomen. We were all crowded by the side table in the dining room. Ruth had cleared the space and scrubbed the surface clean before laying down a plastic sheet. We were dressed head to toe in aprons and masks, and I insisted that we each wore a pair of rubber gloves. And, as we three giant human beings leaned over the tiny sleeping gerbil, I reached for the scalpel and with the smallest blade made a minute incision, as 153 gerbils watched on.

Sadly, all three of Shirley's babies never made it into the world alive. By the looks of things they'd been dead for over twenty-four hours and were shrivelled like peanuts in their shells. Fleur wiped a tear with her sleeve and both Ruth and I battled to remain unaffected. I spayed Shirley while she was still asleep and set her on course for an uneventful and speedy recovery. When she was stitched back up, Fleur threw her arms around me and clung so tight I didn't think she was ever going to let go.

Chapter Five
The Boy, the Rabbit and Me

It was a Thursday night and the surgery was relatively quiet; a few things that could be treated with simple phone advice, one or two drop-ins, but nothing like the mad rush on the weekend. We saw a dog that had been involved in a fight, and a five-month-old German shepherd who'd been vomiting for five days.

The dogfight was as bad as it got. It wasn't so much a fight as an attack. The victim was a Staffordshire bull terrier, who had been out on a walk minding her own business, when she was set upon by Labrador cross. Clearly no one had told her that bull terriers were meant to be the tough ones. It wasn't until her owner pulled the other dog off that the damage stopped. He had carried her, bloodied and injured, the half a mile home and then brought her in to us. She had bite wounds on her leg, neck and ears, and pretty serious swelling.

Some people ask me whether distressed animals affect me or whether seeing it day in, day out deadens the emotional impact. The short answer is that no matter how many times it happens, seeing animals in pain is upsetting but you can't let it get in the way of doing your job. And there's no better feeling than bumping into an owner walking with their dog that you saved from a road traffic accident three weeks before.

We administered injectable antibiotics to keep the bite wounds from becoming infected. I looked at her, lying there, covered in battle-wounds. It's usually Staffies that are cast as the aggressors. As I got to work with suture and an ice compress, it served as a strong reminder against stereotyping breeds.

Lucy, a German shepherd, was up next. She hadn't been responding to the medication she'd been prescribed by her own vet to control her vomiting. I pulled up the skin at the back of her neck to make a tent shape and it was very slow in springing back. She was clinically dehydrated, passing diarrhoea and sleeping for much of the day. There was a lot that could be wrong, so she'd need a full-on clinical investigation. The emergency surgery remit was, as the name suggests, to treat emergencies and prepare them for their regular vet to do anything that could wait until the following day. So we made sure Lucy was comfortable and kept her overnight with an intravenous drip, to be thoroughly checked over in the morning.

I was walking back from the inpatients overnight ward when Harry, an eight-year-old boy clutching a large cardboard box, walked into reception with his mum, Sally. I'd been to Harry's school a couple of times to talk to the children about National Pet Week and Bonfire Night. I love school visits, especially when I take in a special guest – a dog, a mouse, or a snake. My favourite part is the question time at the end; you never know quite what topics you'll end up fielding. At the last school I went to we spent over twenty minutes talking about the proper funeral arrangements for fish.

Harry and his mum turned up at half-past ten with their rabbit, Emily, wrapped in a warm blanket inside a cardboard box. Harry was wearing his red and blue Spider-Man pyjamas, a stripy green bathrobe and slippers. His teeth were brushed, he was ready for bed, but the pained, worried look on his face said that something serious had happened. His mum explained the situation to me.

Harry loved playing with Emily and Emily loved to run around the living room, so when Harry came home from school the first thing he'd do was go outside to Emily's hutch, scoop her up in his arms and carry her inside while Sally got the dinner ready. Emily was a French Lop rabbit. She was a tubby thing with short little legs. She had beautiful long floppy ears that hung down with the tips below her jaw, and her fur was a beautiful sooty-fawn colour with black patches. French Lop rabbits are quite big, so they can be challenging as house rabbits; you need to let them have plenty of space.

Harry would settle down on a beanbag to watch television while Emily bounded and hopped around the living room. Harry made her obstacle courses. He put overturned cardboard boxes, cushions and pillows on the carpet, and carefully placed a line of carrot batons from the start to the finish to mark the route. Harry found it hilarious to watch her hop around the carpet and would score her as if he was judging a TV dance competition. Unlike Bruno Tonioli, however, he spent most of his time trying to fish the competitor out from under the sofa and get her back onto the course. Emily would sit on his lap while he had dinner, and Harry would feed her the vegetables he didn't want. And before Harry went up to the land of nod, he'd carry Emily back to her hutch and say goodnight.

But that evening when Harry walked into the living room, Emily was lying unconscious on the floor. Next to her was a frayed lamp cord and her mouth was still around the wire.

A cardboard box with a mop of floppy hair and two red Spider-Man legs walked into the consulting room. Harry insisted on carrying it with the flaps up so he could see inside. His mum guided him in with a hand across his back and helped him settle the box on the table. It was the first time

Harry tipped his head up. He looked up at me and his eyes filled with tears and emptied on his cheeks.

'Don't worry,' I said.

'I'm so sorry,' he said to me, as if I were a rabbit too.

'It's not your fault,' I told him. 'This happens all the time.'

He wiped away his tears with the sleeve of his pyjama top. As I lifted Emily out of the box and studied her frazzled face I looked into Harry's eyes, and I saw myself in his shoes, a little boy standing exactly where he was, in a veterinary surgery in Stanmore, north-west London.

'When I was your age,' I said, squatting down to his level, 'I had a tabby cat called Suzy. Boy, did we get up to some mischief.'

I put Emily on the table.

'Really?' he said.

'Lots of trouble, yes,' I said.

'Like what?' said Harry.

'I can't tell you with your mum here,' I whispered.

Harry grinned from ear to ear.

'Let's take a look at her,' I said.

While I checked his rabbit's eyes, Harry scuttled round the table to get a better look. Emily normally scrabbled about in the box and wrestled with the vet. So when Harry saw her still and quiet, he pursed his lips.

'Don't worry, Harry,' I said. 'She'll be fine. She's had quite a shock, that's all. Does she play in the living room a lot?'

Harry looked at his mum, then back at me and nodded his head. Usually when advising clients to 'proof' their houses it's regarding a new puppy or kitten; naturally curious, fluffy youngsters who can easily land themselves in trouble if not adequately protected. But with the recent and continuing huge increase in owners choosing house rabbits over dogs and cats, I find I'm giving the 'rabbit-proofing' speech more and more – especially in the run-up to Christmas when fairy lights can be potentially lethal.

'Suzy-cat and I used to play all around the house like you and Emily,' I said. 'You just need to be extra careful with rabbits because they'll nibble just about anything. Their favourite thing is wires. Emily can play in the living room; you just have to make sure the wires are hidden away, or thread them through some plastic tubing – you can get that from a hardware store.'

Harry hung on every word I said. He looked at his mum. She nodded.

'He wants to be a vet when he grows up,' said Sally, ruffling her son's hair.

'Well, you can help me now then,' I said. 'Do you want to come round here?'

The corner of Harry's mouth picked up and he shuffled towards me. I asked Harry to hold Emily's bum while I opened up her mouth.

'Good job,' I said.

Ruth passed me a torch.

'We use this to have a good look around,' I said. 'There we go.'

I didn't take long to locate the affected area.

'Ruth, can you take over from Harry? I think I'm going to need his opinion on this one.'

Harry walked round to where I was standing.

'Hold the torch,' I said. 'Now have a look inside while I keep her mouth open.'

Harry gripped the torch and shone it around his rabbit's mouth like he was investigating a sea cave.

'Can you see in there?' I said.

Harry nodded.

'What can you see?'

He shook his head.

'Can you see that she's burned her tongue?'

He screwed up his eyes and looked at it. He wrinkled his brow.

'She hasn't,' he said.

'She has,' I replied.

'Why isn't it black, then,' asked Harry, 'if it's burned?'

His mum laughed. 'It's not a piece of toast, Harry,' she said.

Harry looked up at us and then began to laugh. He tipped back his head and laughed and laughed. Which got us all going. Then he suddenly stopped laughing and looked at me. 'Is it bad?' he asked.

'It's not great,' I replied. 'She'll be a bit sore for a

few days, but it'll heal. I'll give you an antibiotic and a painkiller which you can give her.'

'Like Panadol?' he asked.

'A bit like that,' I said, 'but in bunny-sized quantities.'

Harry smiled as he pictured what that would look like.

'I've got a joke,' he said.

'Go on.'

'Why are there no painkillers in the jungle?'

'I don't know, Harry,' I said.

'Because the parrots eat them all. Get it?' he said.

'No,' I said. I genuinely didn't.

'Parrots-eat-em-all, silly,' he said.

'Very good,' I laughed. 'Now, Harry, we need to talk about feeding. Burns can take several weeks to heal. And if a rabbit doesn't want to eat, she won't eat.'

Harry's eyes went wide again as he took in every word.

'Try her on food as soon as possible,' I said, 'but she may not take any. If she doesn't, then you'll need to syringe-feed her.'

'I don't have a syringe,' said Harry.

'I can give you one,' I smiled. 'Ruth, will you fetch a fairly big syringe for Harry?'

'I don't like needles,' said Harry.

'Oh, there's no needles,' I said.

'Then how do I inject her?'

Sally chuckled. 'We're not injecting her, Harry,' she explained. 'We'll feed her food. In her mouth.'

Harry thought we were joking. 'Squirt it?'

'That's right,' I said. 'Get some baby food, or liquidize some vegetables, and feed her a small amount with a syringe.'

Harry nodded. 'Did you remember that?' he said to his mum.

Sally smiled. 'Yes, Harry,' she said. 'Let's not take up any more of Mr Abraham's time.' She held out her hand. 'Thank you so much for helping us.'

'No trouble at all,' I said, shaking it. 'Come and see us again.' I picked Emily off the treatment table and put her back in her box. 'And thank you, Harry, for helping me out,' I said as he held out his arms and I passed him the box. 'Now, if we get busy with animals and I need some help, is it OK if I call you?'

Harry looked at me over the cardboard box and his eyes went huge.

'Really?' he said. 'You're serious? Do I get my own outfit?'

'Of course,' I said.

'Then, yes,' he replied. A great big smile twisted from one ear to the other. I wished them both a safe a trip home and led the way out to the car park. I stood by the window and watched Harry buckle the cardboard box into the back seat and lift the flaps to check Emily was OK. He turned and waved to me as they pulled out into the road, and they were gone.

Chapter Six
An Emergency Run

'What sort of night are we going to have tonight, do you reckon?' It was a few weeks after Harry and Emily had come in, and Ruth and I were getting ready to start our shift.

'I just hope it's not a quiet one,' said Ruth. 'I'm not ready to start the *Friends* box set over again.'

On reflection 'I hope it's not a quiet one' was a foolish thing to say. It was one of those lines you catch coming out of your mouth that usually precedes an evening from the pit of hell. In fact, if you played the scene back, I bet you would be able to hear the snide tone of the voice-over man saying something like, 'Be careful what you wish for'. I didn't see any television cameras, but it was one of those surreal evenings where you expected Jeremy Beadle to pop out from behind a bush and tell you it's a great big wind-up.

* * *

Cecilia is one of those names that isn't very common nowadays. I happen to think it's a sweet name, and when it popped up on my computer screen, I smiled. But that was until the biggest dog I have ever seen came into the consulting room.

Cecilia was an Irish wolfhound with the stature of a small pony. Had I been naming her, I would have started with something like 'Jumbo'. She was grey and her coat was shaggy and wiry, and she had a fantastic bushiness around her eyes, like they were hiding behind Brillo pads. She was muscular and strong, and, had she been able to stand up straight on her hind legs, she would easily have dwarfed me and Mike, her owner.

Mike was a furniture salesman and an amateur football referee at the weekends. He was tall and athletic. He and Cecilia lived in a two-storey town-house. Working in an urban practice you don't see many Irish wolfhounds – they need a lot of exercise so are more commonly rural pets, but Mike and Cecilia were both keen runners, and when he finished work every day Mike would change into his running vest and tracksuit and take her out for a five-mile run, as anyone who has ever visited the Withdean Sports Complex between the hours of six and seven can testify. Cecilia would run alongside him for a while then tear off on her own, race another dog, come back and run alongside for a bit and so on.

Today was pretty much like every other Friday. Mike finished his last sales call and returned home. He left his car at the local garage for its annual service and one of the mechanics gave him a lift home where Cecilia was, as ever, waiting at the bottom of the stairs for him to come through the door. She left him a couple of minutes to hang up his jacket and take off his shoes before shuffling over to ask how his day was, with that 'about time' look on her face. Mike had his banana, got changed and the pair left the house for the walk to the sports complex.

An Irish wolfhound's lifespan can vary between six and ten years. Because of their size, the temptation is to take them out running too young. Then their overstretched limbs can suffer irreparable damage. But when they're Cecilia's age, they can give Usain Bolt a run for his money. Cecilia was three years old and she absolutely loved to run. Mike walked her to the park, then as they came round the final bend he'd let her off the lead. Cecilia was an obedient dog and knew to wait until they were on the grass before sprinting off. She waited while Mike did his stretches and warmed himself up.

At first Cecilia appeared fine. When they were in the house, Mike noticed that she hadn't eaten much but thought nothing of it at the time. But the minute they left the house there were signs that something was wrong. A mile or so up the road, she began to wheeze. At first Mike thought she must have swallowed something strange, that it would pass as she swallowed, but when he finally let her off the leash she just stood there with her head and neck extended. Cecilia was having terrible trouble breathing.

Cecilia's head was extended so that her neck was held straight out and made a straight line with her back. She was drawing breaths like she was having an asthma attack, her chest was caving and it sounded like she was gasping for air.

They had come straight to see us on the way back from the park; Mike still had his water bottle in his hand. He set it down on the table. He was wearing his Adidas tracksuit, and there were beads of sweat on his forehead from exercise and nerves. As soon as I saw her, I knew it was serious.

'Has she ever done this before?' I asked.

'No,' he said. 'It came on really sudden; two hours ago she was fine.'

My first thought was that it was pneumonia, or even heart failure. It can be especially difficult with Irish wolfhounds because it can develop very quickly. One minute they're fine and the next they're definitely not.

'Has she had a cough?' I asked.

'She's been fit as a fiddle,' said Mike. 'Seriously, seriously healthy. No problems.'

'Sometimes they pick up a fungal or bacterial infection after kennel cough,' I said.

I leaned in close to her chest. Another common cause is something getting stuck in the lungs.

Her chest wall was pumping like a pair of bellows.

'Mike,' I said, 'I don't want to alarm you . . .'

'OK,' said Mike, nodding.

'If she has any of these conditions we're going to need to see to it right away.'

'What does that mean?' he said.

'Well first I want to X-ray her to make sure there's nothing obstructing the lungs, but . . .'

'But what?' said Mike.

I got out my stethoscope and knelt down beside Cecilia so I could listen to her lungs. The sound of healthy lungs is clear, but what I was hearing were crackles, like the sound of Velcro, a sign that there was fluid in the lungs.

I raised my head and looked at him. With a normal-sized dog an X-ray is never a problem, but with a dog that weighs more than most adult human beings, Cecilia was far too big for our clinic's X-ray table.

In moments of crisis, Ruth is a complete genius. She had walked into the treatment room to check up on us, to find Mike leaning with both arms on the Formica desktop, desperately trying to hold it together, while I racked my brains to think of some way we could X-ray Cecilia. The problem was the equipment we had was designed for animals much smaller than an Irish wolfhound.

'Maybe we could try it anyway,' I'd said.

'It won't work,' Ruth insisted.

So I asked her to get on the phone and try to find us a facility for larger animals. Ruth sprinted down the corridor to reception and started leafing through Gloria's address books. She tried the animal hospital just a little out of town, but their machine was the same as ours. She phoned the university, but couldn't find anyone who was still around. There was one place in Brighton with a facility large enough. It probably wasn't used to requests like ours, but there was nothing to lose. So, with her best telephone voice, Ruth made the call, then came running into the treatment room.

'We're in,' she said. 'If we hurry.' Ruth was out of breath herself now.

'In where?' I asked.

'Brighton General,' she said, panting.

'Brighton *what*?' I said.

'General.'

'The hospital?' asked Mike.

'Yes,' she said. 'I called the switchboard and was told that the duty radiologist would call me back after being bleeped. Which he did, and luckily he loves dogs, too.'

We were all crowded round my tiny car.

'There's no way we'll fit all of us in,' said Mike.

'It's not far, we can squeeze in,' said Ruth. 'Help me with the back seats.'

We opened the boot and set to work, pushing the buttons on the tops of the seats to push them flat, and clearing the junk out of the boot. We laid a blanket down to make things more comfortable for Cecilia. I wasn't sure we were going to get her to lie: she was still standing with her neck extended to help her breathe. With stroking and calming words we managed to coax her into the boot, and with a little encouragement she lay down.

'You OK?' I asked Mike.

He nodded.

'Buckle up,' I said. 'It really isn't far.'

'It's only a mile up the road,' said Ruth. 'They know you're coming.'

Mike buckled himself into the passenger seat and I skirted round to the driver's door. There wasn't enough room for Ruth, and I wanted Mike to be there.

When Ruth closed the boot it acted like a sound box: the wheezing was amplified. I reached for my seat belt and put the key in the ignition, turning it to the right to start the engine. But nothing happened. I turned the key back and tried again. Nothing. I could see out of the side window that Ruth was already halfway back to the practice. I looked at Mike and made a nervous smile, pulled the key right out, shook it, and inserted the key again. Paused for a second then turned it firmly to the right. Still nothing.

'Oh, no,' said Mike, staring straight ahead.

'I'm not sure what's happening,' I confessed.

I looked up at the rear-view mirror and saw Cecilia staring back.

'What now?' said Mike.

'We'll get there,' I said.

The air firing in and out of Cecilia's lungs was harsh and wheezy. Suddenly there was a loud knock to my right; I turned to see Ruth's knuckles rapping on the side window. She opened the door.

'It won't start?' she asked.

I didn't have to answer.

'Don't worry,' she said, 'it's not far. Let's use that.'

She pointed over by the wall.

My eyes travelled to where she was pointing. I looked over the wall and beyond, expecting to see a taxi, or something – anything. But there was nothing.

'What?' I said.

'There.'

'What?' I said again.

'The Sainsbury's trolley,' she cried. 'Come on. It's only half a mile.'

She ran over to the wall, grabbed the abandoned trolley by the bar and dragged it over to us. I laid a piece of hardboard over the top of the trolley while Ruth nipped inside to get some more blankets for cushioning. That was the easy bit. *How do you lift an Irish wolfhound?* Cecilia weighed over a hundred kilograms. We opened the boot and reached in. Mike put his hands under her stomach and forelegs and I supported her rear end. It took several minutes and a lot of repositioning before we were able to lift her enough for Ruth to get her hands under Cecilia's middle. The crackling sound of the air fired in and out of her lungs. The poor dog was fighting for breath. Somehow we managed to get her onto the trolley, and laid a couple of thick grey blankets on top, so she was covered from her chin to her feet. We had her positioned so that her head was at the end that I was pushing. Ruth volunteered to take the front of the trolley and Mike ran alongside talking Cecilia through it. We came out of the car park and turned right, flying down the street.

I could never have foreseen how much her weight would inhibit the motion of the trolley. The trolley was so overloaded it handled like a galleon. They're not the easiest things to steer at the best of times so you had to make sure you were setting off in the direction you wanted to go; you couldn't manoeuvre it if you tried. It took both me and Mike leaning our full weight and pushing hard to get the thing going. We were tearing along the road like a bobsleigh team. Ruth guided the front with her hand locked round the basket, yelling at anyone in her path to get out of the way. They stepped aside as we clattered by, with the sound of racing wheels on tarmac and shuddering metal.

Brighton General Hospital is a huge late-Georgian building that was built as a workhouse and infirmary in the nineteenth century. As we clattered round the final bend of the road the hospital's clock tower came into view, with its domed roof that looks like a pepper pot. The car park was ludicrously busy when we got there, as you would expect for Friday night. We weaved in between cars and pedestrians. The tarmac had an incline and we hadn't gathered quite enough speed to keep the momentum going, so Mike dropped to the back to help me push, tugging the left-hand side of the trolley to steer us out of the way of a BMW.

'Cover her face!' I shouted to Ruth as we slowed our sprint down on approach. Ruth took the ear of the top blanket and pulled it over Cecilia's head, allowing her a little space to breathe. We came to rest at the entrance.

'Where now?' said Mike.

'Stay here,' Ruth told him. 'I'll run in and sort everything out.'

We pulled up outside the electric doors and Ruth ran up to the counter. The waiting room was packed. There were mums and their sons with bandaged heads, old men in wheelchairs, smart women, scruffy drunks – all of them clutching a tiny slip of coloured paper with a black number printed on it, indicating their place in line.

Ruth came charging out of the doors. 'OK, we can go straight through now,' she said.

'Where?' I said.

'In there.' She pointed to where she'd just come from.

'With a shopping trolley?!'

Waiting for us in the ambulance bay was a proper hospital trolley with two porters. It took all four of us to transfer poor Cecilia from our makeshift wheels and whisk her straight through A&E and into the radiology department where she was X-rayed.

We were done and back at the clinic within the hour, clutching fantastic black and white films of her lungs. It brought the confirmation we needed that there was no foreign body in her lungs, no dangerously enlarged heart.

We kept Cecilia overnight on an intravenous drip and started her on a course of antibiotics. Within three weeks she was fighting fit again, tearing around like she always did, and waiting at the foot of the stairs for Mike to come home for his run. It would have made a very nice ending if I could have said that I'd bumped into Mike and Cecilia while I myself was out running in the park, but I'm afraid to say, I'm no runner.

Chapter Seven
They Go 'Moo'

When I was fifteen, our class was sent on a week of 'work experience'. I write this phrase in inverted commas because I always failed to see how a week sitting around twiddling thumbs, photocopying things that probably didn't need to be photo-copied, or reordering book shelves in order of pub-lication can ever be classed as experience of actual 'work'. It seems to me that in any profession there are a list of jobs that are not performed by any-one other than people on work experience, to the extent that the firm of accountants that I was assigned to had a work experience folder in their filing cabinet with lists of unseemly jobs for who-ever was given the dubious honour of filling that role for the week. We all returned to our school desks the following week and filled the class in on what we had been up to. I shared a table with

Thomas White, who had spent his work experience at a marine biology institute in a submarine. He was a nerdy computer kid, and I'd never had cause to be jealous of him before, but when he got out his photographs, I cursed the fact that my dad was friends with Steele, Land & Partners and not Steve Zissou.

Now I was determined to give our work experience boy, Dan, some stories to share with his classmates. Dan had come into the practice a few weeks before to discuss doing work experience with us and seemed keen enough, so I was happy to take him on.

'Change into scrubs,' I said when he arrived for his first shift. 'Ruth will show you where to pick them up.'

Dan played prop in rugby, and his shoulders almost touched both walls of the corridor as he went to the cloakroom to pick up his outfit. He walked back into the consulting room decked out in surgical scrubs, grinning like he'd just been given the ultimate fancy-dress outfit.

Ruth came into the consulting room with a list of patients on her clipboard.

'You've got a cocker spaniel called Max,' she said.

Max staggered into the treatment room. He was a two-year-old spaniel with a beautiful black and tan coat, but he could barely stand up on his own four feet. Max's owner was a mumsy woman in her fifties. She was the outdoors type with trendy wellies, a quilted gilet and a string of pearls around her neck.

I held out my hand. 'Marc.' I introduced myself.

'Joan,' she replied.

'I hope you don't mind if Dan watches. He's on work experience.'

Joan nodded. We got to work.

Max was incredibly bloated. He looked like he'd been inflated with a bicycle pump. Even his cheeks were bloated. He staggered over to the wall and flopped down.

'Uh-oh,' I said.

'Is he drunk?' Dan piped up. 'He looks drunk.'

I threw Dan a glare and he covered his big mouth with his hand in an 'oops' kind of way.

'I'm sorry,' I said to Joan. 'He's not been here

very long.' I turned back to her dog. 'He's very bloated, isn't he? What's the matter with Max?'

'Have a smell,' she said.

I knelt beside her dog and even when I was only halfway down I could smell the fumes rising up. There is no other way of putting it: Max reeked of booze.

'Whoa,' I exclaimed. 'What did he do?'

'He's drunk like a sailor on his first leave,' Joan said.

Dan made an 'I-told-you-so' face.

'He'll eat anything,' Joan told us. 'I was baking a batch of little rolls and left them up on the table. That was at four-thirty. Then I went out to pick up our youngest from her violin lesson. When I got back, Max had eaten half a kilo of fresh yeast dough.'

'Which fermented in his stomach,' I nodded.

If you've ever baked bread, you'll know that the dough likes a warm, moist place to rise. A dog's stomach is a very nice warm, moist place, and the dough can expand to several times its original size, which stretches the stomach and causes pain. It rises as the yeast ferments. The fermentation results in alcohol, which causes toxicity. Not only is this uncomfortable, it can be incredibly dangerous.

'I Googled it,' said Joan, 'and came straight here.'

At that moment Max burped. It was a loud, almost human belch. The burps were what you'd expect from a drunk tramp on a bench.

'He's been doing that on the drive over,' said Joan. Then, dropping her voice to a whisper, added, 'And farts.'

'Wow,' said Dan. 'That's impressive.'

'The farts smell of baked bread,' she said. 'Like you're at an actual bakery.'

I tried to remain professional, but I couldn't help smiling.

'Is it serious?' asked Joan.

'He'll be in a lot of discomfort. And when it comes to ingestion toxicity it can be dangerous,' I said. 'But from what you're saying, with the amount of dough he has eaten, he's going to be OK. We can either give him something to induce vomiting or wait for the bread to work its way out.'

Joan nodded.

'We should give him something for his symptoms, though. His stomach's going to be hurting. Do you have any Pepto Bismol?'

The surgery was quiet after Max and Joan left, which meant that we had a lot of time to sit and chat. Dan was a real talker which, though wearing, was a relief, as to my mind there's nothing worse than constantly having to think of how to keep a conversation going.

Dan was slouching on the sofa, hi-tops on the table, munching from a bag of Doritos.

'What was it like?' he asked.

'Was what like?' I said.

He pushed the bag of crisps in my direction.

'Vet school,' he said. 'Did you always know you wanted to do this?'

'Be a vet?' I replied. 'Yes, but I wanted to work with big animals at first.'

'Like what?' he said.

'Well, I spent some time in Kentucky, with horses. That was interesting. But, I don't know, I was never great with farm animals at vet school.'

'What do you mean?' he said.

Ruth was doing a wheel pose. This is when you bend your back over so your tummy is in the air, your hands are flat on the floor, and your head is upside down.

'Tell him about the cow,' said a strained voice from her red face.

I rolled my eyes. Dan smiled.

'What happened with the cow?' he asked . . .

It was in the middle term of my first year at university that we were each sent out on placements to work with veterinary practices in Midlothian. I was down to work in a rural village practice, which primarily worked with farm animals. I had only lived in London and Edinburgh at that point, so my experience with the countryside had been limited to family holidays in Devon and Somerset, where the closest I had been to a cow or a sheep was as close as any typical rambler gets.

I was dropped at the practice where I would spend the week, bright-eyed and excited. I met an elderly vet at the door with bushes of grey hair covering fifty per cent of his face. His name was Terry. Terry wasn't in scrubs and white tennis shoes, which are nowadays my working wardrobe; he was dressed in a tweedy jacket with a soft-chequered shirt topped off with a flat cap. I looked down at my shiny blue scrubs and wondered why I hadn't been warned about the dress code. The vet looked at his watch as if to make a point. It was barely nine o'clock.

'We country bumpkins keep different time to you soft city folk,' he said. 'Get in for eight in future. You ready to go?'

I nodded keenly. 'Pleased to meet you, sir.'

He grumbled something in reply.

I clambered into his Land Rover, which was splattered with mud right up to the roof. I made small talk and asked about the size of the village, the size of his caseload, and if there were any good pubs in the area. Terry didn't say very much to me, and when he did ask me questions I found myself shifting uncomfortably.

'Have they taught you much about cows?' he asked.

'Cows?' I said.

'Cows. You know, they go moo.'

I couldn't tell if he was joking with me, so I just made a sort of snorty laugh.

'I suppose I know a fair amount,' I said.

'All right, here we are,' he said. 'Let's find out, then.'

We pulled up at a dairy farm. There were hundreds if not thousands of Friesian cows dotted around the surrounding hills. It looked like a still from a Müller yoghurt commercial. The ground was muddy with tractor tread and littered with deep ruts now filled with dirty brown, sometimes oily puddles. Terry swung open the Land Rover door and squelched onto the ground. I shook my head as I tried to find somewhere soft to land but slurped into the mud up to my ankles.

'I see you've bought George Clooney,' said the dairy farmer when we walked into the shed. I hoped it was a reference to my good looks but it was probably a reference to my immaculate blue outfit, which was more suited to *ER* than a filthy cattle shed. The farmer sat on a barrel and looked me up and down.

Terry rolled his eyes. 'He's with us for a week. Go on, Marc, you do this one,' he said.

I had expected that I'd be getting my hands dirty at some point during the week, but not in the first half-hour. I stepped forward. Terry and the farmer raised their eyebrows.

'Pleased to meet you,' I said. 'What are we here for then?'

The farmer looked at me and said, 'I want to know if she's pregnant.' He gestured to a huge black and white cow in one of the stalls.

'Pregnant?' I said, gritting my teeth. 'Cool. Well, let's see.'

I looked at Terry for some sort of cue, but he just stared right back at me.

'I need to get a few things from the car,' I said.

Terry threw me the keys and took a seat on a hay bale next to the farmer. I trudged out of the shed. I didn't turn back to see their faces but I'm sure he shook his head as I walked away.

I wasn't quite sure what I needed from the car – this was a cunning stalling tactic. The trek back bought me some crucial minutes to think things through. I had been at the husbandry lectures and I knew we had been taught about this, I just had to find the appropriate place in my memory where I had stored the information. We had been through everything theoretically in the classroom and I knew my way around a cow – at least, a nice black and white diagram of a cow. But learning something on paper in a light, state-of-the-art lecture facility in Edinburgh is very different from actually doing it in practice on a squelchy farm in the countryside, especially when it's a procedure like this. *Pregnancy. Cow pregnancy.* I ran through the lectures in my head, mentally going over the notes, visualizing the diagrams. There it was. To diagnose bovine pregnancy or check for an infection, you've got to reach into a cow's rectum and feel for the uterus, ovaries and Fallopian tubes. There's no substitute for getting up to your elbows in warm, gooey innards. *This is just a test to see what I'm made of,* I thought to myself, *but one thing I'm not is squeamish.* When I got to the Land Rover I looked inside the medicine bag for arm-length rubber gloves. Then I closed my eyes and muttered a prayer.

* * *

I took a deep breath before I stepped back into the cow shed. My heart was literally pounding; I'm sure the farmer's wife could hear it from the kitchen. I stood outside, just out of sight. Terry and the farmer were chuckling. When I stepped in, they fell silent.

'OK,' I said, rolling the right sleeve of my shirt above the elbow. 'You all right?'

The two of them nodded.

'Get on with it,' Terry instructed.

The cow was huge. I approached her slowly from behind. Her stomach was massive. Her tail swished from side to side. I shuffled slowly forward so as not to startle or frighten her and very gently placed my left hand on her back. Her tail swished from side to side again. Was that a happy swish, an angry swish or a mildly irritated swish? My mind started to race. How would I know what to feel for? I mean, what do ovaries, cow ovaries, feel like? How on earth do they expect you to learn this kind of thing in a lecture hall, anyway? I rested my head on my left arm as I felt around with my right, my gloved hand patting down directly below the tail. I went further and further down until I found the hole and inserted my hand. I went in as far as my elbow, the warm gooey innards pressing against my skin. I felt a surge of adrenaline, my heart was pumping. I had my arm in her rectum. And then I felt a hand on my shoulder. I looked round to see the farmer with his head in his hands. To see Terry's hand on my shoulder. I followed it up his tweed jacket to his face. Terry shook his head.

'That's the wrong hole, my boy,' he said.

He looked so disappointed with me. I stepped back and he stepped up, and the farmer patted the vacant hay bale next to him. That more or less marked the beginning and the end of my time as a large animal vet.

Chapter Eight
Siamese Twins

One – or rather two – of the practice's more colourful clients were sisters. Amber and Amanda were identical twins. Middle-aged and single, the pair lived in an apartment a stone's throw from the surgery. I have never been one to stereotype, but Amber and Amanda were eerily like characters dreamed up in the fantastic imagination of someone like Tim Burton. They were exactly what you would imagine identical twins to be. They were the identical height, they had identical faces, they were dressed identically, their hair was identically coiffed. With Amber and Amanda it was almost as if they were not two different people at all, but one – they just took it in turns to talk. And it was almost as if Tim Burton had delivered them scripts in the morning post, and hid himself somewhere just off camera to whisper stage directions into their ears. The cherry on the cake was Amber and Amanda's choice of pet: Siamese cats.

Dan was trying to teach me a card game when the twins arrived. They rushed in with Bella, one of their three Siamese. The poor cat had collapsed at home with what we suspected was a massive heart attack. I peeked in the top of her carrier and saw the beautiful animal with her warm grey fur lying on the bottom. She didn't move a muscle and her huge almond-shaped eyes were wide open. Dan hung back by the sink and watched. He may have been a wisecracker, but it wasn't difficult to read the gravity of the situation. I reached in and felt the left-hand side of Bella's chest to see if I could detect a heart beat. The best place to feel a cat's pulse is on the femoral artery that runs along the inside of the thigh. One of the twins clutched the other's hand. Dan rested the sole of his foot against the back wall. I withdrew my hands and looked at them.

'Amber and Amanda, would it be OK if you wait in the other room for a few minutes?' I said.

They both stared at me with that same look of incomprehension. I held their gaze long enough that they would understand. The news wasn't good. I watched their lips quiver.

'I just want to make a few checks,' I said. 'It's best if I do that here. I'll get Ruth to help you.'

I left the consulting room and walked down the hall to the office where Ruth was certain to be. It was only about twenty or thirty strides to the office, but long enough to allow me to snatch a breath from the tension in the other room. I hate delivering news like this. Ruth was on the telephone. I walked over and stood behind her. She twisted round when she heard me enter and read the bad news in my face.

'Sorry, love, can I call you back later?' she said.

Ruth put down the phone.

I sighed. 'There's no vital signs,' I said. 'Could you take the ladies into the other room and make sure they've got a cup of tea?'

Ruth nodded.

'I'm just gonna do some checks.'

Ruth went to the consulting room and led the

twins away. When I walked back into the treatment room Dan was sitting on a chair, his chin resting in his hands. He opened his mouth to say something, then thought better of it.

I picked Bella's limp body out of the carrier and gently put her on the table. After I laid her down I ran my hands over her tummy. She was bony over her back and had what appeared to be a plump tummy but was actually an enlarged liver with fluid accumulation in the abdomen. This poor cat must have died of sudden heart failure or Feline Infectious Peritonitis, which is a chronic wasting disease.

'Has she gone?' asked Dan.

I looked at him and nodded.

'There's fluid in her chest. I want to take a sample so we can find out why,' I said.

Failing hearts can't pump enough blood and allow some of the liquid in the blood to leak into the lungs. It's called pulmonary oedema. When this fluid leaks out and surrounds the lungs themselves it can make breathing extremely difficult and uncomfortable.

Ruth stuck her head round the door. 'Are you all right?' she said.

She was carrying two mugs of tea. I nodded.

'I'll, er, I'll come through in a minute,' I said.

I went over to the supplies cupboard and found a syringe and needle. I inserted the needle into Bella's chest and drew out an amount of fluid. It was clear and watery. I repeated it a few times until I had successfully removed a fair amount of liquid from in and around her lungs.

I peeled off my gloves and threw them into the bin. There's no easy way to tell somebody that their beloved pet has died. People often ask me what to say in that situation. There really isn't a simple answer. Often people feel that when their pet has died they have lost a family member. And it's a sad fact that there is nothing we can say that will make the mourning process any easier. One of the best ways to help someone cope with the loss is to reassure them they are not alone. Offer to help out with arrangements. If their pet is being cremated, perhaps offer to pick up the ashes for them. Or even send them a condolence card.

Dan got up from his seat and started to follow me out.

'Sorry, mate,' I said. 'They'll probably prefer it if there are less of us there.'

Dan nodded. 'Cool,' he said. 'I'll wait here.'

I stood outside the door for a second and took a deep breath, sucking the air in through my nose, holding it there, then blowing it out again. I counted to ten.

When I walked into the waiting room, the atmosphere was black. Ruth was sitting beside Amber, with a hand on her knee. Amanda had her handkerchief out, clenched tightly in her hand. None of them looked up. I wandered over and sat myself down in the seat next to Amanda. What do you say? What *can* you say? The twins looked at me, desperately wanting to hear something good. I followed their eyes as they tightened their lips then looked down at their laps. I leaned forward and put a consoling hand on Amanda's shoulder.

'There's no easy way to say this,' I said. I paused. 'We did all we could. I'm so sorry.'

I wished I could have let them know that Bella

died peacefully, but with that much fluid in her lungs she would have been in a lot of discomfort. I wished I could have lied and told them it was otherwise, but I couldn't, so there was nothing more to say. We just hung in that moment. A tear rolled down Amber's cheek and dropped into her mug.

'She's gone to a better place,' said Ruth.

The twins nodded.

Suddenly there was a loud noise, a yelp from down the corridor.

'Oh my God!' the voice yelled. 'Oh my God!'

We all looked up as Dan came screaming into the room. His eyes were wild and his arms were trembling. I raised my eyebrows in a way that said, 'Come on, Dan, surely this could wait'. What had possessed him? Surely he could read the situation. But Dan had seen something he absolutely had to share and he could barely get his words out.

'She's breathing!' he gasped. 'She's breathing!'

Ruth leaped from her seat, the twins looked completely baffled.

'That's impossible,' I said indignantly.

'Come and see if you don't believe me,' said Dan.

Normally I would have insisted the twins stay behind in the waiting room while I went to investigate the re-diagnosis of a work experiencer, but this wasn't a normal situation.

We hurried into the treatment room and, sure enough, Bella had come round. I couldn't understand it. All the signs of death had been there, and yet here she was with her eyes blinking, slowly stretching her legs like she was waking from sleep. Amanda and Amber burst into tears as Ruth stretched forward and stroked her fur. I looked at Dan, who was grinning from ear to ear and pacing about excitedly. He couldn't stand still. All I could think was that Bella had been impossibly close to death but removing the fluid from her chest had allowed her to breathe again. She must have been hanging on by the thinnest of threads. I'd never seen anything like it. I looked at the people standing in the room, witnesses of this miracle and my clunking misdiagnosis. It was marvellous on one hand, but utterly unnerving on the other. I fished about for something to say, but I couldn't come up with anything.

'It's a miracle,' said Ruth hugging the twins together.

And it was. Their faces were radiant, stretched by two enormous identical smiles. Again, I tried to say something, but my tongue went fat in my mouth.

Amber and Amanda came up to me, each taking hold of my arms.

'We're so glad we came to you,' they said.

I tried to agree with them. I wanted to agree with them, but under it all I was thinking, *Why are you so glad you came to me? I've just told you your cat is dead, and she's clearly not.*

So instead I beamed a great big smile back as we all bathed in the moment when Bella the Siamese came back from the dead. As the twins stroked Bella's belly you could hear the tiniest, feeblest purr emanating from inside the cat I had thought had died.

I hate to try to read too much into events, but if there is a moral in Bella's story, then it is this:

never believe that you know more than you do, never think you're better than you are, and even when you think you've seen everything, always leave room for the unexpected.

There was a big cheesy grin plastered all over Dan's face for the rest of the day. He'd played his part in a minor miracle, and I discovered that behind his joking was a caring soul. He wasn't here on work experience because he had nowhere else to go. He loved people and he loved animals, and what we had just witnessed was a priceless example of what happens when those two worlds collide.

Chapter Nine
Special Delivery

My social calendar revolved around coffees in cafés, and drinks in pubs with friends who had the afternoon off or who had sneaked in a late lunch hour. I was catching up with a friend I hadn't seen for a couple of months in a new bar that had opened under one of the old arches at the beach-front.

We caught up as old friends do. He asked me about the practice and I gave him the warts-and-all rundown. James kept shaking his head and making these sighing sounds.

'It sounds amazing,' he said.

'What does?' I said.

'You know,' he said, 'to be providing such a valuable service. But boy, I couldn't do the hours. Don't you ever wish you had some time off?'

'The hours are a lot,' I admitted, 'but I do get

time to relax. Afternoons, for a start, and it's not like I'm always on duty.'

James wasn't eating but I ordered chicken with green beans and dauphinoise potatoes. I never know quite what to order in the afternoon. Strictly it's my breakfast slot but it's also my lunch, and I've never been one for brunches. I tend to err on the side of two lunches per day if given the opportunity. The waitress brought us our drinks and a few minutes later out came the food. I was just cutting into a slice of melt-in-your-mouth potato when a lady ran up to our table and pounced.

'There you are!' she exclaimed.

The lady was in her seventies. She was wearing a faux-fur coat. She had a pearl set, bright red lipstick, and her hair was coiffured like a Hollywood star's.

'Hello,' I said, with a mouthful of chicken, somewhat taken aback. I didn't recognize her at all. James's eyes went wide and he leaned back in his seat to take it all in. I looked to him for support. He looked back at me like this was something he believed happened to me every day.

The lady grabbed my arm. 'We saw you walk past our window, Doctor Abraham, so I beetled down to find you,' she said. 'And thank God I did!'

A whiff of Chanel perfume blew over us both.

'Prudence has gone into labour!' she said.

'Who?' I said.

'Pru,' she repeated. 'Come on, it's an emergency.'

'I'm so sorry, but—'

'Come on,' she said. 'Please?'

I looked down at my half-eaten chicken, at the untouched green beans and the creamy potatoes, and then back up to the elderly lady tugging on my arm. James beckoned over the waitress.

'Can this be put into a takeaway box?' he asked.

A doggy bag may have been more appropriate.

James looked at me with a flicker of excitement in his eyes. 'Come on,' he said, 'let's not hang around. Er, do you mind if I come along?'

Prudence was a Pekingese. The Chinese breed is over 2000 years old. Whilst nowadays the Pekingese are considered toy dogs, they were once believed to have originated from the Buddha himself, and

Skipper, the yellow Labrabor, aged 10 weeks

Me in the surgery with Bailey, the Cavalier King Charles spaniel

Spending time with cute puppies is all part of the job!

This cat has found an unusual way to travel . . .

Some patients can be a bit prickly!

*Poppy – the chocolate Labrador – lived up to her name
with her appetite for chocolate Santas!*

Emily the rabbit – after making a full recovery

Can you spot Bundle, our practice cat?

This poorly pup was sick with an incredibly contagious disease (parvovirus) when he came to see me . . .

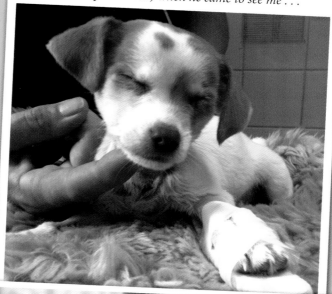

. . . but happily went on to make a full recovery

*Although in this book Chickens
turned out to be a dog . . .*

*. . . I've treated the real thing
in my surgery, too!*

Talking to school kids is one of my favourite parts of the job

served primarily as a temple dog. This has paved the way for many myths and legends. The most popular story tells how the Pekingese was the off-spring of a lion and a marmoset. The legend has it that a lion and a marmoset fell in love, so they went the Buddha for help. He allowed the very big lion to marry the rather small marmoset, but only if he surrendered his height and his might. The Buddha allowed the lion to shrink to the size of the marmoset but keep possession of his lion's heart and character. From this came the Pekingese, or so the story goes. There is another version of the story where the lion falls in love with a butterfly, though this seems even more implausible.

The lady who stole us away from our lunch was called Marjorie. Prudence belonged to her neighbour, Phyllis. They lived in apartments on different levels in a beautiful Regency building, as close to the beach as you can get. I'd say 'within spitting distance' but Marjorie and Phyllis were not spitting types. When we arrived outside their apartment building I saw that the most striking features were the huge floor-to-ceiling windows behind black wrought-iron balconies that flowed around the side like the levels of the *QE2*. It looked similarly luxurious and similarly iconic. Marjorie's apartment was on the first floor and Phyllis lived above her. They were the best of friends. Both widowed the same year, the 'girls' made a pact that they weren't leaving this world without a fight, and were going to live as full and rich a life as possible. It's actually nice to live on your own, Marjorie told me, when you know you've got someone so close by. They even had a code. Two rings on the phone meant 'Pop down if you fancy'. Two rings in reply meant 'See you in five'.

Marjorie's apartment was stunning. It was the sort of home that needs a baby grand piano, if only as a place to display one's silver-framed photographs, as the mantelpiece is *so* common. On Marjorie's piano I counted seventeen frames. Most were filled with smiling children, but the large one in the centre had a sepia photograph of her late husband standing by a Spitfire. The front room was stunning. It was the sort of room that wouldn't suit the name 'lounge'; it befitted something more grand like 'drawing room', the perfect place for day-dreaming over a cup of well-brewed tea.

'Marge!' yelled Phyllis from the study. 'Did you find him?'

'Right here!' she called.

James could barely contain himself. He leaned in and whispered in my ear, 'I should hang out with you more often.' Marjorie tugged the sleeve of my coat and dragged me towards a pair of mahogany concertinaed doors. I was marshalled past the balcony from which, Marjorie pointed out, they'd spotted us walking. We were a good few hundred metres from the beachfront promenade.

'You must have incredible eyesight!' I said.

Marjorie pointed towards a pair of binoculars sitting on top of a copy of the *Daily Telegraph*, folded to the crossword page, of course. The mind boggles.

Pru was a golden Pekingese. When we walked into the study she was lying on her back on a poofy cushion that Phyllis had tucked behind her. Phyllis was kneeling in front of her and swivelled right round so she'd see us as soon as we came in the door.

'Oh, Doctor Abraham,' she said. 'We're awfully, ever so grateful.' She clasped her hands together and tilted her head at an angle. 'Marjorie and I were going spare. Oh, I say, another dashing gentleman,' she added.

'Hi,' began James, 'I'm—'

'A nurse,' I said, before he put his foot in it. 'We trained at college together.'

'What luck!' she said, and rose to her feet so we could get a good look at Prudence. For all my joking about the lion and the marmoset you had to admit it was a fitting description. She had a beautiful double-thick golden coat that flowed from her broad black face. Her eyes were round and dark, her nose short and broad with these large open nostrils. Prudence was a beautiful dog. But she was in a protracted labour.

Canine labours can last any time between six and twelve hours. In the first stage, the mother will exhibit nesting behaviour and, as with cats, her body temperature will drop. The animal often appears restless. Stage-two labour is characterized by active uterine contractions. In this stage, the puppies are usually born within two hours of each other. Prudence had started second stage labour with good, strong contractions, but two hours had passed and there was no water bag or puppy. When three hours went by she'd started crying with each movement. I had always planned to go straight to the surgery after my lunch with James so luckily I had my stethoscope with me in my bag and my emergency kit in the car. As I moved the cold steel of the stethoscope around Prudence's tummy it seemed there was a part of the puppy presenting, but I couldn't make out what. It wasn't a leg or a head; maybe it was the neck?

A Caesarean was almost inevitable. My car was ten minutes' walk away, six minutes if we pegged it. I had a quiet word with James and we decided a taxi might be the better option if we could get one immediately. I sent him straight down onto the street while Phyllis went to fetch some towels. With emergency Caesareans, you typically want to get in there as soon as possible. Nevertheless, anything we could do now would save valuable time when we got to the clinic. Before we make an incision the dog's belly is shaved. So I asked the ladies for a razor. Marjorie disappeared off to the bathroom. She was away for some time: you could hear her opening and closing cabinets and turning out the cupboards. Eventually she ran back in, pulling a razor out of a packet and juggling a can of shaving foam.

James came tearing into the room. He was short of breath. 'There's a cab outside,' he said, breaking off to gawp at me kneeling by Prudence with a razor in my hand. Marjorie had wrapped her tightly in a towel to keep her warm and let her know everything would be OK. I took my time and finished the shaving, washing the razor with a flourish in a Pyrex jug of warm water that Phyllis had set down.

We got to the practice in record time. I'd put a call in to Gloria and asked her to prepare the theatre. There was a nurse on hand and pretty much everything we needed. Gloria didn't say a word but gave me one of those sunny smiles that says, *It's all gonna be fine.*

I wasted no time – I was already down to my T-shirt before I was in the front door – got into my scrubs faster than one of Madonna's costume changes and whirred into action. After Pru was happily anaesthetized and her breathing tube inserted, I made a mid-line incision and pulled out the uterine horns.

When the uterus was open we discovered the single puppy with his neck extended over the pelvis and his front legs bent backwards at the shoulders. Puppies cannot be born in this breach position. We removed him and I closed the incision with internal stitches so the puppy wouldn't be bothered by the knots when he was suckling. Put like that, it sounds like a quick job, but you have to be incredibly careful and it took around fifty minutes.

While I was working on the stitches, the nurse took on Pru's role of keeping the new puppy breathing and making sure his airways were clear, and James took on my job of keeping Marjorie and Phyllis amused with quips and jokes. Baby Christopher, the most adorable Pekingese puppy, with his tiny little legs and his pink snout, had entered the world.

Chapter Ten
The Assembly

It was a Thursday morning and we'd finished the shift, but the night, or rather the day, was far from over. There was that rare thing on the wall calendar: an entry, and for the morning too. In big black letters I had scrawled *Assembly*. I was going to visit a local school.

'How do I look?' I asked Ruth.

She looked me up and down.

'You look great,' she said sarcastically.

I scowled.

'Well, what am I meant to say?' Ruth said. 'You're wearing scrubs, you wear them every day. I mean, what should I comment on, your shoes?'

She had a point.

I met Miss Gilmore, one of the teachers, in the road outside the school. I had suggested we met in the car park, but she said she didn't want to give the game away. She'd told the children that they had a very special visitor and they were excited.

'I feel weird about this surprise,' I said. 'They're going to be crushingly disappointed when *I* step out on stage.' I opened the car door and took out my winter coat. It was bitterly cold. My breath made clouds in the air as I zipped my coat up over my uniform. 'They're probably expecting a footballer from the Albion or something.'

Miss Gilmore explained to me that there were approximately 400 pupils aged between three and eleven, and they were divided into fifteen classes, each named after a different bird, from starlings to kestrels and penguins. At nine o'clock on the dot a buzzer would sound and one by one the classes were called to the assembly hall.

I sat at the front of the hall on a raised stage, hidden by a curtain. Then came a sound like a polite herd of elephants that had been told to walk, not run. I peeked out from behind the curtain. There was a scrum to sit at the front. As soon as the pupils got through the door, the 'Walk, don't run' rule went out the window – they waddled, jostled, skid and slid as quickly as they could to nab the best patches of floor space on which to park their bottoms.

Within five or six minutes the room was full. I'd visited individual classes before, but I had never spoken to a whole school assembly and I wasn't prepared for the sound of a hall brimming with children.

Miss Gilmore stepped onto the stage. 'Good morning, school,' she said in a loud, teacherly voice.

'Good morning, Miss Gilmore,' they chimed back in unison.

'We have a very special guest today. Before I introduce him, does anyone have any idea who it might be?'

A forest of hands went up.

'Before I choose one of you, I'm going to give you a clue. Think about what event is coming up this weekend, and ask yourself what professional person might be coming in to give some very important advice.'

The arms dropped. Then one by one the arms went up again.

'I'm going to take three guesses,' she said. 'Jane.'

A little girl in the third row back looked to the left and to the right and realized that Miss Gilmore meant her.

'A witch,' she tried.

There was an intake of breath.

'Not a witch,' said Miss Gilmore. 'Halloween was last week.'

There was a collective sigh of relief.

Miss Gilmore pointed to another child.

'A pumpkin,' said Tommy.

The whole hall burst into fits of laughter. Tommy looked pretty pleased with himself and collected his pats on the back with a grin.

'Sensible answers, please,' said Miss Gilmore.

She pointed to a little girl sitting quietly in the front row. She was easily dwarfed by everyone else, but stuck up her hand as high as it would go.

'Lucy,' she said, 'who do you think it might be?'

All eyes turned to Lucy. She looked coyly at the

floor and wound her finger into her skirt. Then in the softest of tones, she said: 'I've forgotten.'

Miss Gilmore shook her head. 'All right. Well I'll let him introduce himself then. Put your hands together for Doctor Abraham.'

I got up from my plastic chair, came out from behind the curtain and walked to the centre of the stage. The whole room gasped. Four hundred pairs of eyes were staring at me in my greeny-blue scrubs.

'Good morning, everyone,' I said.

'Good morning, Doctor Abraham,' they sing-songed back.

It was a little more subdued than I had expected, but perhaps I should have been quicker to reassure them that I wasn't a dentist. Dentists wear a similar uniform and I am sure half of them were terrified to open their mouths.

'What day is Saturday?' I asked.

'Guy Fawkes Day,' said a smart-looking boy in the front.

'That's right, and what's so good about fire-works night?'

I picked a sweet-looking girl with her hand up.

'Burning stuff!' she said.

They certainly were cute.

I gave the usual talk about checking for hedge-hogs in the garden when they got home, and then it came to the matter of pets and fireworks. Every child in the room had something to say on the subject. I have never met a child who doesn't have a question or a story about animals and I was starting to relax into it. I had figured out from speaking to individual classes that the trick was to ask questions, make it interactive. I wasn't sure if that would work in an assembly but it seemed to.

'OK,' I said, 'now this is the really serious bit. Are you all listening? I want you to turn to the person on your left and right and say, "Listen, this is important!"'

The kids did as I said and the hall floor bubbled with excitement.

'Who here has a pet?' I asked.

Across the room hands popped up like mush-rooms.

'All of those with your hands up, does anyone know what you should do with your pets on Bonfire Night? I'll give you a clue: fireworks can be very loud!'

Three rows back a boy's arm shot into the air and he groaned like he was in pain. I could have picked anyone but this kid looked like he would pass out if I didn't choose him.

'OK,' I pointed to the boy. 'What's your name?'

His eyes went wide. 'Scott,' he said.

Scott was about seven or eight, with a wild crop of blond hair.

'What pets do you have?' I said.

'I have a cat called Oscar,' he told me. 'He's a white one.'

'A white one?' I said, 'Very nice. So, Scott, what should you do with Oscar on Bonfire Night?'

'That's easy,' said Scott. 'Take him to the bon-fire.'

The hall broke into laughter again. Scott looked quite annoyed. He stuck out his bottom lip.

'Why would you take Oscar to the bonfire?' I asked.

'Because it's really, really cold outside,' he said, 'and cats are warm. I am warm, Oscar is warm and a fire is warm. Together we'll all be really warm, and we won't even need to put on our coats!'

Chapter Eleven
Christmas Is Coming

I love the Christmas build-up. It was the first week of December and we were in the middle of a cold snap. The roads were clear as I drove into work and the rain was lashing down. The little wipers of my car were breaking their backs to swish the water left and right. A lady ran across the road with shopping bags filled with toys and games. I let out a long sigh. *Hello, Father Christmas, it's nice to have you back.*

Ruth was up to her festive best. She had a Christmas tree earring in one ear and a red parrot one in the other. Apparently she'd spent her last Christmas in Peru and she wanted to be transported straight back there when she caught her reflection in the bathroom mirror.

'You should wear a paper crown,' she told me,

'cover up your baldness.' She wound a length of tinsel around in her hair.

'Take that off,' I said.

'Why?'

'Because you never know who we might have coming in today. I don't want you talking to a distressed owner dressed up like a Christmas tree.'

Ruth didn't reply, but she unwound the decorations from her hair and tied them to the standard lamp in the waiting room.

'Scrooge!' she grumbled under her breath.

Things ramp up at Christmas. Around the festive season when there's turkey, presents and parties on the brain, pets are often the last things we think about. It's understandable, but we always try to remind owners of a few basic things, like anchoring the Christmas tree so it doesn't topple over, covering up electric cords and flashing fairy lights, keeping holly and mistletoe out of reach, and the one that lots of owners forget: don't hang chocolate decorations from the tree.

June was something of a supergran. She'd taken

early retirement to help her daughter out with her two sons. I have never seen two children with so much energy. I suspected that they were half human and half Tasmanian devil. Everywhere these boys went they left a trail of destruction behind them.

June looked after the boys after school while her daughter finished her shift at the BP garage. That night, June had popped out to Tesco to pick up a few essentials leaving her next-door neighbour to watch the boys, and when she got back, the kids were worked up into a frenzy. June was weighed down with heavy shopping bags, two or three in each hand. The boys waited by the door to pounce. As soon as they heard the key in the lock and saw the handle go, they grabbed her by the arms and pulled her towards the kitchen.

'Hey!' said June, taken aback. 'Stop it!'

They were tugging on her hard.

'STOP IT! What's got into you?'

'Poppy's died!' the boys said.

June's heart stopped beating.

* * *

Poppy was June's chocolate Labrador, and the love of her life. When Alf, June's husband, passed away, the family bought her the most beautiful, thoughtful puppy you could picture. Full of life and with boundless energy, Poppy was so much more than a pet and the boys totally adored her. She was always doing something daft: she'd chew everything she could get her paws on – remote control cars, mobile phones, DVDs, even slippers.

'She's under the Christmas tree,' they said. 'Come quick.'

Leaving the front door wide open, June dumped her carrier bags and ran in, milk and eggs spilling everywhere. The living room was fairly small and the Christmas tree was ginormous. It was one of those trees that was so big you had to saw the top off to fit it in, and even though it had only been indoors a few days it was already dropping needles. Under the giant tree, where the presents would soon be, lay Poppy, stretched out and motionless, with a big swollen belly.

'Poppy!'

The boys stood over by the door and looked like

they were about to cry. June crouched down by Poppy's side and stroked her belly. She noticed that the branches above her were totally bare. Poppy was lying on a bed of pine needles. There were foil wrappers littering the carpet and only a handful of chocolates still hung on the higher branches.

'She ate the chocolates, didn't she, Gran?' the boys said.

June turned round and slowly nodded her head.

Poor Poppy had munched her way through thirteen chocolate Santas still in their coloured foil wrapping.

'We saw her licking her lips for ages,' the boys said, 'and then she started to cry.'

It was high drama when they arrived at the practice. Poppy couldn't walk; her back legs buckled when she tried. With help from June's neighbour they had carefully carried the tubby puppy over to the back seat of the car and driven straight over without even telephoning. One of the boys sat in the back and whispered encouragement into her ear, the other rode up in the front, wrapping his head round the seat to watch. We heard the commotion before we saw them. June came bursting in. 'Can someone help me with my dog?'

We dropped what we were doing.

Ruth and I followed her out to her car. The boys were squabbling in the back. Poppy was crying. June's phone went. I caught snatches of the conversation: 'I'm at the vet's . . . Poppy's eaten chocolates . . . The boys are here . . . No, they didn't do anything . . . Chocolate . . . it's poisonous . . .'

I took Poppy in my arms and carried her across the tarmac and into the practice.

'How many do you think she's eaten?' I asked.

June pulled a face.

'There were twenty in the pack, I think,' she said.

Chocolate may seem a trivial thing, but to dogs it can be deadly. As humans, we just think it'll harm the waistline and rot our teeth. To dogs, chocolate is equally moreish, but potentially lethal. The toxicity of chocolate for dogs is due to its theobromine content, a chemical in the cocoa bean that is similar to caffeine. And if you think posh chocolates might be better, think again. Those

Green and Black's dark chocolate bars may be organic and tasty but they're stuffed full of theobromine. Because chocolate looks so harmless, as opposed to something like rat poison, it's easy to overlook it as a threat. That's how it has become one of the most common poisonings to occur in pets, especially at Christmas and Easter.

Symptoms like this usually present between six and twelve hours after ingestion, so it was likely Poppy had just fancied something sweet to nibble on after her lunch. You'll usually witness some degree of acute abdominal pain followed by explosive diarrhoea, but in the most severe cases there could be fits or even a one-way coma. I've heard of fatalities from dogs eating a large amount of chocolate and going untreated. A vet in my last practice witnessed two such cases. In both instances it took little more than a handful of chocolates. Deaths amongst large dogs left untreated are not in any way uncommon.

'Has Poppy vomited?' I asked.

'I don't think so,' said June. She looked at the boys. They shook their heads.

'Tremors or spasm?' I said.

'No.'

I listened to her lungs: the breathing was quick and irregular. It was a good sign that Poppy wasn't fitting – a convulsing dog would need to be immediately admitted to intensive care for heavy sedation. My main concern was to get as much of the poison out of Poppy's stomach and give her something to slow the absorption of the toxic substances into her intestines.

We gave her an apomorphine injection to induce vomiting and then put her on a drip. It wasn't long before poor Poppy repeatedly vomited up various puddles of partially chewed and digested chocolate all over the hurriedly put-down old newspapers. She was lucky June brought her in before the symptoms worsened. Poppy was going to be fine.

'Well done for bringing her in so quickly,' said Ruth.

'Don't thank me,' said June. 'Thank the boys. They were the ones who spotted something was up.'

I looked around the room.

'Where are the boys, out of interest?'

It didn't remain a mystery long.

There was laughter coming from reception, and not an adult laugh. It was the laugh of two pre-pubescent hyenas. June went charging out. Ruth and I exchanged glances. We counted to ten. Then the air filled with the blood-curdling scream of a grandmother coming to the end of her patience.

'KYLE!' she yelled. 'GET OUT OF THE FILING CABINET!'

Chapter Twelve
A Fox in the Cold

It felt like a classic case of déjà vu. Ruth and I were in my car, the night shift was over, and we had one last stop to make. We crossed the same traffic lights, waited at the same junctions and turned down the same roads into a quiet residential street, where, unbeknownst to all but a few, Brighton's foremost husband-and-wife animal-rescue double-act lived. We pulled up outside and parked behind their little blue Metro in the drive. The one with the large seagull sticker on the rear window – the emblem of the football club they loved, and the bird that was a recurring theme in their lives. We stood outside on the front doorstep, rubbing our hands together to keep them warm.

'Look at me,' I warned Ruth. 'You may be about to see some gerbils. So no cutesy noises, no mushy stuff, no goo-goo-ga-ga nonsense, all right?'

Ruth nodded.

'I'm serious,' I said. 'We have a reputation for professionalism to uphold.'

Fleur opened the door. She had two baby gerbils in her hands.

When Ruth caught sight of the newborns, the baby gerbil faces peeking out of Fleur's hand, she completely and utterly melted.

'Awwwwwwww!' she squealed. 'Wook at their wittle noses.'

Fleur was beaming. I wasn't.

'Ruth!' I sighed.

'I can't help it,' she said. 'I'd been mentally preparing myself to see *one* gerbil all the way here in the car, and then there's two of the little bundles. *Two*. Aren't they the most perfect wittle thwings?'

'Yes, they are – aren't you?' said Fleur, ever so gently stroking their heads with the tips of her fingers.

I stood on the doorstep, shaking my head.

We weren't here for the gerbils this time. Roger had received a late-night phone call from a lady down the road with an injured fox in her garden. A lot of injuries to wild animals occur around this time of year, either road traffic accidents in country lanes when drivers aren't paying attention, or problems with litter. In the party season households create more waste. Homeowners may not think twice before they throw out huge numbers of bottles or cans, boxes or polystyrene that can be hazardous to curious animals, and in towns and cities streets are filled with pint glasses and discarded beer cans.

Roger was in the kitchen eating Marmite on toast. The counters were full of crumbs and the knife was lying on the side with a buttery trail smeared behind it. The morning radio show was in full swing, which was a little disorientating for us as we'd just finished our 'day' and were ready to go bed.

'Good morning, Marc,' he said between mouthfuls. 'And you must be the famous Ruth.'

We shook hands. Roger was a big man, which surprised me when I first met him, probably because Fleur was so small. He brushed some crumbs off his mouth with the back of his hand.

'Thanks for coming out. The lady's just down the road. I didn't want to move him in case it's worse than it looks,' he said.

'It's a fox?' I confirmed.

Roger carried his plate to the bin and scraped off the leftover crusts with the side of his knife.

'A young cub. Can't be much more than a year old. It's not a pretty sight. It looks like she's been hit in the eye by a firework,' he said. 'Makes you want to cry.'

It was a short walk to the neighbour's house. Roger and Fleur grabbed their coats and a torch, and the four of us walked along the pavement of the quiet cul-de-sac like a crack SAS choir of carol singers on an early morning reconnaissance mission.

Their neighbour, Julie, was an animal lover too. Though feeding foxes is generally frowned upon, she couldn't help but leave out scraps of food and water for the fox family who walked along her fence and stopped off in her garden. They'd visit in the early evening and the little cubs played in the grass, scrapping and howling and tumbling. But

Julie noticed that something was different this week, and when she came out in the morning to take away their dishes there was an orange ear peeking out of a cardboard box by the tool shed – an orange ear that belonged to a little fox cub, shivering in the rain.

Julie was waiting for us at the front door. She was tall and cheery, the sort of person who looks right at you when they talk. She wore a big baggy sweatshirt with Daffy Duck on it, grey and softened through hundreds of washes and tumbles. Julie was a single mum. She had a son called Danny on the severe end of the autistic spectrum whose best friend was their cat, Charlie. Charlie was more than a pet, he was Danny's best friend; when Danny wouldn't talk to Julie, he'd talk through Charlie. Julie said she spent hours every week sitting outside Danny's door, eavesdropping on the conversations he had with their cat. It was often the only way she could find out how her son was really doing, whether he was being bullied again at school and what other kids had said to him. Danny was upstairs playing computer games when we got there. Julie led us into the hallway and called up the stairs.

'The vet's here, Danny,' she said. 'I'm just taking them out to the shed.'

She lingered at the stairs for a minute with her hand on the railing.

'I doubt he'll come down,' she said to us in a hushed voice. 'He doesn't do well with strangers.'

'What games does he play?' I asked her.

'Oh, war ones, mainly,' she said. 'He plays other people around the world on the internet. He can't see them, you see, so it's easier. You can pretend to be anyone you want.'

We walked through the living room, past two empty bowls of cereal and kids' cartoons on television, and out through the double doors into the garden. There was a short paved patio that turned into a narrow strip of grass that stretched a long way, and running around the perimeter was a high panel fence. Julie wasn't the gardening type; it seemed like she dabbled but only did the bare minimum. The grass went from well-kept lawn to knee-high in the space of fifteen metres. At the top end by the house were pots of perennial plants, but as the garden sloped down the flowerbeds became increasingly overgrown and brambles crawled everywhere. Right at the bottom of the garden was a tumble-down shed and a pile of branches.

It was hard to see anything in the early morning light and we only had one torch. We walked in single file with Julie leading the way and Ruth and me behind. Roger and Fleur smiled as we were steered round an old wheelbarrow that was concealed by high grasses. Julie held the torch and occasionally the light beam flashed against things, and we saw stuff we hadn't noticed before. There were feeders in every conceivable place: bird houses nailed to trees, and pine cones hanging from tree branches that Julie told me she'd spread with peanut butter then rolled in bird seed – a slap-up feast if you've got a beak.

'I was brought up in the country, you see, and I like to be near the wild. Cities give me the shivers. I'm sorry. I keep the garden like this deliberately so it's a bit wild, to encourage all sorts of visitors.

Every day I wake up and hope there'll be a deer, but it hasn't happened yet.'

We walked on a bit further and then the pace slowed. Julie told us to be quiet as we approached the tumble-down shed. We were looking for the cub. We stopped a couple of metres away, and Ruth and Fleur dropped back so we wouldn't overwhelm her.

I couldn't see her at first. It was hard to pick out much.

'Over there,' Julie whispered, gesturing towards the gap between the shed and the fence. There was an old cardboard box. It must have been outside for a while: the cardboard was wet and soggy and there was a hole torn, or perhaps bitten, in the side. Roger and I crept up and as we edged closer we were able to look inside. At the bottom of the box, curled up like a shrimp, was the terrified fox cub. Julie had brought down a blanket and the little creature had wrapped herself inside it with only her face peeking out. The fur on her head was matted and wet. In the opening of the box were two dishes, one filled with cat food, the other with a single piece of white bread, and the tiniest puddle of milk. As Roger bent down and moved slowly towards her, the fox cub turned her head, and I saw for the first time the state of her right eye.

We were now a couple of metres away. Usually you wouldn't be able to catch a fox but this one was so sick she just lay there. The golden rule is never to approach an injured wild animal like a fox: they have needle-sharp teeth and can bite when nervous. Roger was wearing protective gloves for this reason. He sent me round the other side of the box and we gradually closed in.

'It's OK,' Roger repeated under his breath. 'It's OK.'

The cub was crying. They were quiet, mournful cries. A fox cub usually cries when it's hungry, but this cub had been like this for hours and her parents were nowhere to be seen. I peered in through the side of the box: the whole right side of her head was inflamed and her eyelid was lacerated. The socket was swollen and infected, but her cornea was ruptured, with the iris prolapsing out through the hole. Roger whispered my name and

I looked up to see his hands stretching out and reaching towards the cub. We had tranquillizers with us but it didn't look as if we'd need them. Sometimes when you see footage of young wild animals it's hard to see them as anything other than a creature from the world of Beatrix Potter, but foxes should be thought of in the same way as cats; they can leap and bite at any moment, especially when scared. Their claws are fiercely sharp. Roger told me later that he usually catches a fox with a net, or cubs with a blanket or a thick coat. Darkness is reassuring for the fox; it is a nocturnal animal and it helps them feel safe and comfortable.

Roger scooped up the cub in a bundle of blanket, and slipped a muzzle on her like he'd done it a hundred times, and with the cub in his arms we turned quickly and walked back towards the house. As we reached the patio I saw Danny's face appear at the window, pushed up against the glass.

At the back of Fleur and Roger's house were two long buildings. One was a converted garage, the other a long shed. I say shed, but it was so much more than that. It was a permanent wooden room with windows and a carpet, and inside there was space to house and rehabilitate injured animals. It was bright and clean; there was a sink over by the window, and a long treatment table. Roger had latex gloves and swabs and ointments, and along the floor by the wall was a line of carriers and cages. Roger wasn't a veterinarian, though; he only did basic rehabilitation, and the cub's condition was far worse than he could treat. She would need to go to hospital for surgery. Usually, as an emergency vet, I'd refer her, but I was well aware that Roger worked out of the kindness of his heart and had to foot the huge medical bills himself. Roger carried the cub over and laid her on the treatment table. We huddled around the blanketed bundle.

'Thanks for your help,' said Roger. 'I'm sorry to have called you out. I just thought it was smart to have you along in case something else was wrong. I'll drive her to the hospital.'

He stood over the fox cub and I could see him counting the cost of the hospital treatment. I looked at my watch: it was almost nine o'clock; we were officially off duty.

I beckoned Ruth over and whispered in her ear. 'Are you free for the next couple of hours?'

Her eyes lit up and her lips parted into a smile.

'Let's do it. I'll get the box of tricks,' she said, and she disappeared off to the car.

We thought 'Holly' would be a good name for the fox cub because we found her at Christmas time. The procedure took just over an hour. We had to remove her eye and stitch her eyelids together. We put her on a course of antibiotics and anti-inflammatories, and gave her a buster collar to wear to stop her scratching the wound. It's always sad to see an animal lose an eye, but Holly would manage just fine with one and still be a perfectly active vixen. I've performed the operation on several dogs. Even totally blind dogs manage very well in familiar surroundings and they're never bothered by only having one eye once it's healed.

Roger was over the moon.

'You guys,' he said, 'are angels. Let me get a

picture of you two with Holly for the website.'

We crouched down by the treatment table as Roger rummaged in a box in the corner for his digital camera.

Ruth put her arm round me. 'This has been one of the best years of my life,' she said.

I didn't know quite what to say.

'Say cheese!' called Roger. 'After three . . .'

Just as he said it Ruth tipped back her head and let out the most almighty yawn. You know how infectious yawns are. Ruth managed to compose herself by the time Roger pressed the button, but for ever now, frozen in time and preserved on the world wide web, is a photograph of the two of us: Ruth, beaming ear to ear, and me with a great big mouth-cave as if I was catching flies.

Epilogue
Merry Christmas

I worked through the Christmas weekend, waiting by the phone for emergency calls, while families up and down the country played charades, yelled at each other and slept off the turkey. We had sorted out a rota. Ruth had the weekend off to spend with her family, and then I was with mine for the next couple of days so the practice was always covered, but it meant it was just me on Christmas Day, watching movies and Christmas specials, eating a takeaway pizza (turkey, naturally) with my feet up on the practice sofa. It was quiet, eerie and reflective. But then, that time between Christmas and New Year is made for that sort of thing. Routines stop and you step out of real life for a little bit. Most often this takes place at home with other people around; people who know you best, your family. There isn't that much to do apart from eat, drink, catch up, play games, and think about life and what you're doing. But for me that year, the reflective time started in the office. The silent waiting for the phone to ring. The knick-knacks pinned to the corkboard. The cards I'd kept above my desk. I'd built that place – I did it.

I woke up on Boxing Day morning still in the same place on the practice couch. My overnight bag was on the chair. I brushed my teeth in front of the bathroom mirror and stared at the man looking back at me. As I drove out of the car park I turned over the events of the year in my head. I thought about the first day with the new partners, about meeting Ruth, about the biker with the budgie, Chickens the rattling golden retriever, Mrs Lopez and the cat who laid the egg. I thought about Fleur and her gerbils and the Siamese twins. It had been nothing if not a roller-coaster ride.

The passenger seat was covered with gifts; you could barely see the fabric: a large box from Ruth, a bottle of something from Gloria. I hadn't known them a year before but they were like family now. But before I got on my way to the place I used to call home, there was still one small visit to make.

It was a short drive. I pulled up outside the house and reached into the glove box. I pulled out a present I'd wrapped up the night before in shiny red paper. I was dreadful at gift-wrapping so the whole thing was done up in metres of tape. I sat in my seat and looked at the house. The lights were on, the place looked warm. There was a Christmas tree in the window with dancing lights, and two sets of wellington boots standing patiently by the front door. It was a perfect picture of Christmas. I stood outside and rang the bell. There were noises from inside, footsteps getting louder, then Julie, Danny's mother, opened the door. She was wearing an apron and oven gloves and did a double take.

'Marc! Hello, Marc. What a surprise! Happy Christmas!' She gave me a hug and said, 'What are you doing here?'

'Just dropping something off,' I said. 'I got a little gift for Danny.'

Julie's eyes went wide. 'For Danny?'

'It's just a little thing,' I said, 'but when you

talked about him . . . well, anyway, I thought he'd like it.'

I handed over the gift, a war game for Danny's computer.

'Happy Christmas from me and Holly the fox.'

GLOSSARY

Airfix, p.49 — Manufacturer of plastic scale model kits.

apomorphine, p.128 — Type of drug that when injected into the skin makes a dog vomit.

autistic, p.134 — A developmental disorder, characterized by a limited ability to communicate.

Caesearean, p.48 — Surgical procedure to deliver a baby.

cardiac arrest, p.22 — Failure of the pumping action of the heart.

caudal aspect, p.9 — Rear part of an organ, closest to the tail.

cornea, p.138 — Transparent front part of the eye, in front of the iris and pupil.

dentition, p.21   Related to the development of teeth and their alignment in the mouth.

digestive tract, p.21   The stomach and intestines – parts of the body used for digestion.

enteritia, p.21   A disease commonly associated with budgies. Symptoms include lethargy and diarrhoea.

femoral artery, p.93   General term comprising the two large arteries in each thigh.

foreign body, p.10   An object originating outside the body.

gastric torsion, p.8   Common in large dogs, the distention and twisting of the stomach due to excessive gas content.

gastrostomy, p.11   A surgical opening in the stomach. (Not to be confused with gastro*nomy*!)

husbandry, p.89   The agricultural practice of

breeding and raising livestock.

intravenous, p.11 — Any drug that is administered directly into the vein.

inverting sutures, p.11 — Type of stitch, commonly used in gastrointestinal surgery.

kennel cough, p.69 — Highly contagious canine illness characterized by inflammation of the upper respiratory system.

lesions, p.32 — Any abnormalities in the tissue of an animal.

Lilliputians, p.46 — Tiny people or beings. Originally related to the inhabitants of Lilliput, an imaginary country in Swift's *Gulliver's Travels*.

mid-line, p.11 — Imaginary line that divides the body lengthways into right and left halves.

Read on for loads more information on how to care for your own pets – and top tips on becoming a vet from Marc himself!

How to Look After Your Pet

If you have a pet of your very own to care for, lucky you! Having a pet is like having a best friend – they're always there for you no matter what, and to them, you're the most important person in the world.

But having a pet is also a big responsibility. There are all kinds of things to consider if you want to be a good pet owner. Take a look at the list below to make sure you're doing all the things that will keep your pet happy and healthy.

 If you're about to get a pet, make sure that it's definitely the right animal for you before you bring them home. With bigger animals like dogs and cats, your parents might have to help you take care of them, and you'll need the support of everyone you live with to really make your pet feel like part of the family. If you can't have a dog or cat, there are still lots of other animals that could be right for you. Consider what your house and garden is like, if anyone in your family has any allergies, what kind of home your pet needs – a hutch or a cage – and what time you can commit to caring for your pet after school and at weekends.

Never buy a puppy from a pet shop. Always contact the Kennel Club to find a responsible breeder, and please remember there are lots of brilliant animal companions – including dogs, cats and rabbits – who are looking for caring owners in rescue centres around the country. Your local vet will be able to advise you on the best places in your area, and you can also look online for more information about re-homing mature animals.

 So you have your pet – what do you feed it? It's important to make sure your pet has the right diet to give him or her a long and healthy life. Think of it as giving your animal their five-a-day! Just as important as giving them the *right* food is making sure they don't eat the *wrong* food. If you have any concerns that your pet might have eaten something that's bad for them, visit your vet straight away.

 Just as it is for humans, exercise is really important for animals. Without it, they can become overweight and ill. A dog will need daily walks – and remember, the bigger the dog, the more exercise they need. Smaller animals also need enough space to run around in – make sure their hutch or cage is the right size for them, and if you have a rabbit or guinea pig, consider getting an outdoor cage that gives them space to run around and access to grass when the weather's nice.

 Even if your pet is healthy, you must take them along to the vet for regular checks and vaccination. Lots of animals might need extra care that may be difficult for you to carry out on your own, like clipping nails or bathing. Your vet will be able to help you or give advice on how to groom your pet yourself.

 Preventative treatments to keep your pet healthy are also important. You might need to consider worming or treating your animal for fleas to prevent them becoming ill – your vet will be able to advise you and give you the right medicine for your pet.

 Just like people, animals are social creatures. They need company and interaction to stay happy and healthy. Do as much research as you can to find out what your pet needs. If you have a dog, taking it to a public area like a park can be a good place to meet other dog owners. But also be aware of animals that don't get along – and if you're introducing a new animal into a home with existing pets, be sure you're around to supervise when they first meet, and until they're used to one another.

 One of the best things about having a pet is how much they love to play! Pet shops have loads of toys available for every kind of animal, but you can also have fun just throwing a ball for your dog, or dragging a piece of wool along the floor for your cat – but don't let him swallow it. Make sure you spend some time every day playing with your pet, or giving them a cuddle if they're a small animal.

 Sadly, pets can get lost or go missing – especially ones that have lots of access to the outside like dogs or cats. Make sure that you microchip your pet as soon as you get it – this is by far the best way to make sure you're reunited with your pet should they ever get lost or stolen.

Common Pet Illnesses

Lots of people ask: how do I know if my pet is ill? They can't tell you if they have a pain or when they're feeling sick, so how do you know? Sometimes, if the symptom is external, like a skin wound or a rash, it's easy to tell when you need to go to a vet. But you should also be aware of other more subtle changes in behaviour, like loss of appetite, tiredness or anxiety.

Here are some of the most common illnesses that I treat in my surgery – by getting your pet to see a vet as soon as possible, most of these can be treated simply and get your pet back to full health in no time!

Skin wounds sometimes occur with pets that have access to other animals. Dogs can get bitten if they fight other dogs when out walking and cats often engage in territorial scraps when out roaming the neighbourhood, which can result in bite abscesses. These usually require a good clean up and sometimes surgical repair.

Coughs are common in all animals. Infectious coughs can also be caught from other dogs, the most common being kennel cough. This is a dry hacking cough that owners often describe as sounding like their dog has something stuck in their throat. Lungworm is another cause of coughing that can be caught from dogs eating snails and slugs infected with parasitic larvae.

Vomiting can happen when an animal's intestines are inflamed through infection, or when there's an obstruction that may require surgical removal – for example if your pet has eaten something it shouldn't. Vomiting animals can become dehydrated very quickly and often need to be put on a drip to replace vital lost fluids.

Diarrhoea is usually a result of a digestive disturbance, often brought about when your pet has eaten something that doesn't agree with them. Like vomiting it can also be a cause of dehydration so must be treated quickly and effectively.

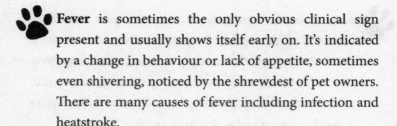 **Fever** is sometimes the only obvious clinical sign present and usually shows itself early on. It's indicated by a change in behaviour or lack of appetite, sometimes even shivering, noticed by the shrewdest of pet owners. There are many causes of fever including infection and heatstroke.

 **Cystitis** is the inflammation of the bladder wall which can be caused by a bacterial infection, or sometimes stones or crystals in the urine. Like in humans, cystitis is a painful disease that often requires a course of anti-biotics to treat effectively.

Lameness – or limping – is usually the result of sudden trauma like a fracture, cut pad, grass seed, twist or sprain, but can also be caused by long term pain such as arthritis. Lame animals often require an X-ray to help assess what's damaged and the best course of treatment.

Conjunctivitis is the inflammation of the inner eyelids which can be caused by a number of things including infection, allergies and blunt or foreign body trauma. Conjunctivitis is often very painful and requires treatment as soon as possible.

 Dental problems can show themselves in many different ways including excessive salivation, weight loss, the animal deliberately eating on one side of its mouth or an obvious wobbly tooth. Teeth problems are common in pets and can largely be prevented by regular oral care, like brushing or dental treats (for dogs). A rabbit's back teeth can wear down unevenly too, requiring regular filing down under general anaesthetic.

 Skin problems usually make the animal very itchy and are commonly caused by external parasites like fleas and burrowing mites, or allergies to pollen or house dust mites. Most parasites can be prevented by routine monthly spot-on preparations, available from your vet.

 Anal glands can present problems ranging from needing routine emptying to impaction and infection. These two small glands are found in every dog's bottom and are used for scent and communication.

Pet Emergencies

Although quite rare, a few pets might require emergency treatment at some point during their life. Being vigilant and aware of any worrying signs in your pet's behaviour is the best way of making sure they are treated swiftly and effectively.

All of the below conditions require immediate medical attention, so make sure you are familiar with your local vet's opening hours and get your pet to them as quickly as you can. If the problem happens at night, call your normal vet who'll have an out-of-hours or emergency vet's number to contact and begin treatment as soon as possible. Looking into what facilities are available in your local area before an emergency happens means you will have the right information to hand should you ever need an emergency vet.

 Road traffic accidents (RTAs) are very serious and can result in death or severe injury. Often bones are fractured and there can be significant blood loss too. Most RTAs will require hospitalization, drips, X-rays and might even need surgery to fix them.

 Caesarian is an operation that must be carried out when the female animal is unable to give birth on her own. In dogs, the most common reason to carry out a

Caesarian is a wrongly positioned puppy in the birth canal causing an obstruction or being simply too big to come out naturally.

Twisted stomach (Gastric torsion) is one of the biggest emergencies vets see and usually affects large, deep-chested breeds of dog, like boxers, Great Danes and Irish setters. There can be many factors responsible for causing this condtion including exercise too soon after a meal or swallowing too much air or food causing bloating. All cases require immediate treatment, stabilisation and abdominal surgery to un-twist and repair the stomach. Sadly this condition commonly happens at night and is only detected in the morning when it may be too late.

Seizures can happen in animals of any age and are caused by disturbances to the brain from poisoning, or may have no obvious cause at all. Most can be success-fully treated if detected early and sometimes lifelong medication is required for prevention.

Flystrike is a terrible disease that commonly affects rabbits during the warmer summer months. It can be avoided with frequent checks to make sure your rabbit's bottom is clean and free from faecal matter, at least twice a day in the summer. This will discourage dangerous flies from being attracted to the rabbit. If you spot anything unusual during your check, get your rabbit to the vet straight away. This disease is especially common in overweight or sick bunnies.

Stroke is usually an indication of heart problems and can range in severity. As with humans, strokes are very serious and usually sudden in onset, which can make it particularly difficult for both patient and owner to come to terms with.

Foreign body (FB) obstruction can be of an airway, (e.g. a tennis ball) or, more commonly, the intestines (e.g. toy, sock or bone). All types of foreign body obstruction require immediate investition and, frequently, surgery. X-rays are usally needed although some FBs don't always show up obviously.

Stitch-ups caused by dog fights or cut pads can sometimes be clipped, cleaned and repaired under local anaesthetic or sedation, but many will require general anaesthesia to fix properly. Assuming there are no problems with healing, the stitches can usually be removed after about ten days.

Diabetic hypoglycaemia describes a dangerously low blood sugar level, suffered by diabetic patients that have usually been given their insulin injection but have not eaten. This sudden dip in blood sugar can cause disorientation and even cause the animal to slip into a coma. Luckily, diabetic hypoglycaemia is extremely treatable with oral or injectable glucose if detected early enough.

Advice for Future Vets!

So, you want to become a vet? Good choice! Being a vet is a hugely rewarding career and seeing an animal you've treated get back to full health is one of the best experiences in the world. But it takes a lot more than just a love of animals to become a vet (although it's a good start!).

Chances are if you're reading this, you're a good few years off having to make the GCSE and A-Level choices that you'll need to be accepted onto a veterinary course at university. However, there are a few things you can start doing now to help your application when the time comes.

Work experience and volunteering is a great way of learning as much as you can about the care of animals. Although lots of places might not be able to offer under 16s full work experience placements, it's still worth visiting with your parents to introduce yourself and see if they need an extra pair of hands at weekends. Places to approach include your local vet, catteries, boarding kennels, riding stables, children's zoos – and even farms!

 If you're working with animals, never be afraid to ask questions – no matter how silly they may appear. Professional vets and animal handlers can give you loads of advice that might one day be invaluable. Learning as much as you can about looking after animals from a young age is one of the best lessons you can get on what it's like to be a practising vet.

 Try to encourage your parents to let you have a pet of your own – if you haven't already. Caring for your own animal and being aware of their needs is a tiny taste of the kind of responsibility you'll have when you're a vet. If you can't have your own pet, then spending time at other places where you can be around animals is even more important. Visiting friends and relatives who have animals is good too.

 Working hard at school is crucial, as vets need top grades to make it onto one of the highly competitive courses to study veterinary medcine at university. Science is especially important – so get studying now!

 Having outside interests and hobbies is also vital to make sure you get one of those all-important university places. Anything from being a member of a local sports team to charity work looks great on applications, and is rewarding as well. Remember that vets don't just deal with animals – they have to talk to the owners too! Being part of a community or team is a great way of learning the communication skills you'll need should you ever have to deal with a difficult pet owner (it happens!).

 There are loads of magazines and websites dedicated to the care of pets. Read as much as you can, especially on those animals that you might not be familiar with. Vets have to be able to treat all animals – not just dogs and cats – so being squeamish about spiders or snakes is not an option!

Take Me Home
Tales of Battersea Dogs

Melissa Wareham always wanted to work with dogs when she grew up – and got her first job at Battersea Dogs & Cats Home, cleaning out the kennels!

Meet Tulip, the mongrel who liked to ride solo on the bus, stinky Pepe le Pew who arrived in need of a wash, and Benjamin, the lucky lurcher who was picked to meet the Queen, in this heart-warming story of Melissa's life working at Battersea Dogs & Cats Home.

ISBN: 978-1-849-41392-3

Norton
The Loveable Cat Who Travelled the World

Peter Gethers hates cats. That is until he meets Norton,
a very cute, very friendly Scottish Fold kitten.

Soon Peter and Norton are inseparable, travelling together
on trains and boats, in planes and cars all over the world!
Eating at restaurants, making new friends and meeting
famous movie stars – read all about these and Norton's
other real-life adventures in this wonderful true story.

ISBN: 978-1-849-41387-9

Meet the naughtiest dogs in the world!

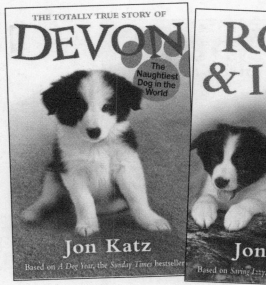

Jon Katz always enjoyed a peaceful life – until his quiet farm became home to three mischievous Border collie puppies!

These two adorable books are packed full of cuddly pups, naughty adventures and wonderful real-life memories. Join in the fun at Bedlam Farm!

The Totally True Story of Devon: 978-1-849-41110-3
Rose & Izzy: 978-1-849-41278-0